JUNKYARD DRUID

A NEW ADULT URBAN FANTASY NOVEL

M.D. MASSEY

MODERN DIGITAL PUBLISHING

Modern Digital Publishing

P.O. Box 682

Dripping Springs, Texas 78620

Junkyard Druid/ M.D. Massey. — 1st ed.

PROLOGUE

Kingsland, TX—Two Years Before the Present Day

I staked the vampire with all my might, pinning it to a live oak tree as it writhed and screamed. With clockwork timing, I ducked, just before Jesse's blade sliced the thing's head clean off. The nosferatu's ugly melon rolled away as I wrenched the stake out and returned it to my combat harness. My partner was already on the move, so I followed her lithe and lovely form up the trail to the cave's entrance.

We'd run into a menagerie of baddies thus far—everything from nos-type vampires to cu sith to giant spiders. Despite their numbers, they were child's play compared to the monster we hunted: Caoránach, known as the mother of all demons in Irish legend. Her "children" had been trying to kill us for the better part of an hour. But instead of thwarting us, like a trail of bread crumbs they'd led us straight to her lair.

We'd tracked the demoness to a large body of water nestled in the rolling Texas Hill Country northwest of Austin. She loved lakes and caves, so to find her, we'd checked the crime stats in her likely hiding spots. The trail of bodies had led us here, to the northern end of Buchanan Lake, where the Colorado River drained into the reservoir. Caves dotted the hills around the lake, and as we'd suspected, some were beneath the waterline. Combined with the steady flow of tourists and anglers who flocked to the area each weekend, the place may as well have been custom-made for a flesh-eating demoness-slash-dragon-slash-water serpent from Hell.

Nearly all the large lakes in Texas were human-made, and those in the Highland Lakes area were no exception. Back in the 30s and 40s, engineers had dammed up the Colorado River in six separate places to control flooding and had set up hydroelectric plants to generate clean energy. At the time, the projects had displaced thousands of people, along with a slew of supernatural creatures.

As I understood it, the government had spent a ton of money relocating the creatures who'd been willing to cooperate. And for the ones that hadn't been willing? Before the monsters could sabotage the construction on the dams, people like us had been hired to take care of them.

Well, not quite like us. We didn't hunt the Unseelie fae and other things that go bump in the night purely for money; we did it because it was my birthright. My family had been at odds with the fae for millennia. Before I'd even come of age, one of the worst of those creatures had come looking for me, to exact revenge for something my ancestor two thousand years removed had done.

It wasn't my fault that Fionn MacCumhaill had been a certified badass, or that his favorite hobby had been beheading monsters. I certainly hadn't deserved a bloodthirsty vampire dwarf, looking to rip my heart out and drain me like a stuck pig, showing up on my doorstep.

Yeah, you'd think a three-foot-tall vampire would've been no big deal.

You'd be wrong.

At the time, Jesse and I had been sophomores in high school. She'd been my best friend since grade school, the one person who'd stood up for pudgy little Colin whenever people had bullied fat and nerdy me. The first day we'd met, she punched a kid's lights out for pushing me around. After that, we'd become inseparable.

Jesse had helped me defeat the Avartagh, the vampire dwarf that had traveled halfway across the world to exact vengeance on the last living heir to the MacCumhaill legacy. And she'd stuck with me over the next few years while "Uncle Finn" had trained us in all manner of minor magic and major violence.

Finnegas wasn't really my uncle, you see. He was the last living druid, more than two thousand years old, and he'd been looking after my family since around 200 AD. For the last several years, he'd trained Jesse and me to hunt every kind of supernatural creature, to beat them at their own game. As far as we were concerned, no glamour could fool us, no magic could hold us, and no fae could outsmart us. We'd slain trolls, goblins, vampires, werewolves, demons, ghasts, and ghouls all across the Lone Star state, and had gained reputations as hunters who got the job done.

This assignment—catching Caoránach—was to be our grand opus, our graduate thesis, the culmination of all our training. Uncle Finn had told us the demoness was still weakened by all the energy it had taken for her to travel back across the Veil, centuries after the last time she'd been defeated. That was the thing with ancient, powerful creatures; you could destroy their physical bodies, but eventually, they'd come back. They might not return for decades or even centuries, but with creatures made more of magic than flesh, you could never rid the world of their presence for good.

I guess that's what had kept our family in business

all that time. I wasn't complaining, because I'd grown to love the violence and chaos of battle, the sheer exhilaration of beheading a monster that could've easily ripped my throat out with one bite or slash of its claws. After experiencing that thrill for the first time, no way was I was ever going back to a mundane life.

Nope, it was the hunter's life for me, and Jesse felt the same way. An athletic, raven-haired beauty, Jess could kick ass with the best of them. We'd bonded over that first kill, and as we'd matured, we'd become more than just friends and partners. We'd spent our nights chasing Unseelie fae through the back alleys and woods of every major city and county in Texas, and our days had been spent in other, equally enjoyable pursuits.

The truth was, it wasn't about the sex—I just wanted to be around Jesse, no matter what we were doing. But if I had to choose, hunting and sexy time *would* be at the top of my list of favorite activities we shared. Tonight's hunt was certainly no exception, and a good hunt always meant even better sex after we were done.

All the more reason to roll this demonic bitch up and send her back across the Veil.

The trail we'd been following led us to a narrow cave opening above a small, hidden cove. Earlier, we'd cast cantrips to enhance our senses, so following the trail was a piece of cake. Jesse stood at the entrance, smiling at me with a look that spoke of mischief and an eagerness to get on with the hunt.

"You ready?" she asked.

"Ready when you are, beautiful."

She slapped me playfully on the ass and spun away before I could return the favor. "Just wait until I show you what I'm wearing beneath all this leather and body armor."

I'd been wondering that all night. We were both dressed in motorcycle leathers reinforced with Kevlar, under level IIIA ballistic vests. The leathers were sort of like modern armor—lighter than chainmail or plate, yet just as durable. Jesse filled hers out like a champ, that was for sure. She was built like an Olympic heptathlete: one part CrossFitter, and two parts collegiate sprinter.

I appraised her hungrily, and I marveled at the fact that I got to spend my days and nights with the most beautiful woman I'd ever known. I was completely smitten with her, and if I ever lost her, I didn't know what I'd do. Unfortunately, I hadn't worked up the courage to tell her that—yet.

Tonight was going to be the night. Once we took care of the Caoránach, I planned to surprise Jesse by taking her to the new flat I'd rented for us in the city. Our parents thought we were leaving for college in the fall, but in truth, we'd planned to move in together and make our living hunting supernatural baddies instead. It paid well—and besides, who had time for things like school and work when you were busy saving the world? Or at least, our small part of it.

I waggled my eyebrows at her, knowing I looked goofy as all hell. "Well then, I guess we'd better hop to it. That demoness isn't going to kill herself."

She snickered and gestured with one of her short swords. "Gentlemen first."

My face split into a broad grin at our running joke. I always took point because I was so protective of Jesse. She let me, even though it was slightly chauvinistic and completely unnecessary; the girl could take care of herself. Regardless, I led the way into the cave with Jesse at my back. And at that moment, there was no place on earth I'd have rather been.

THE PASSAGEWAY REMAINED NARROW, dark, and cramped for several hundred yards. Thanks to our night-vision spell, navigating the pitch-black tunnel was no big deal, and soon we reached a larger chamber. Water dripped from stalactites high overhead, and our boots made squishing sounds on the muddy floor below.

Surprisingly, the cave was stifling inside, even though we were far underground. Even weirder, the deeper we went, the hotter it got. The place had an awful odor: a combination of rotting animal carcasses, human waste, dried blood, and death. Those smells were sure signs we were getting close. Demons loved to torture their victims—thus, the blood, shit, and urine—and often preferred the taste of putrescent flesh. You'd never face a creature with worse breath than a demon.

The stench combined with the quiet had me spooked. Our approach had been much too easy thus far. Besides the monsters we'd killed outside, nothing had halted our progress through the caves. I began to worry we were walking into a trap. Still, I kept my fears to myself. Jesse loved to tease me, and the last thing I needed tonight was to embarrass myself over nothing.

Moving cautiously, we skirted the edge of the enormous cavern. The irregularly shaped chamber had several side grottos, and many large stalagmites blocked our view. Shadows clung to the ceiling and the far corners of the cave, and even with our vision-enhancing magic, we couldn't see everything. Illusory magic was at work here.

Jesse must've been thinking the same thing because she signaled for me to keep an eye on the gloom overhead. Then, with a few more hand signs, she told me we should split up. Totally a bad idea in horror movies; also not a good tactic when clearing rooms with a partner. But, when facing supernatural creatures in large, open spaces, sometimes it was best to make sure your enemy couldn't take both you and your battle buddy out at once. So long as you avoided getting into a crossfire, that is.

Following Jesse's suggestion, I crept around the left side of the cavern, and she took the right. We were nearly halfway around when a small, shadowy form dropped from the ceiling and landed in the center of the room. The creature was humanoid, vaguely female-looking, and cloaked in the same unnatural darkness I'd noticed earlier—and that told me it needed to die, preferably as soon as possible.

Unfortunately, Jesse stood exactly opposite from me on the other side of the cave, and I couldn't shoot from this position without the risk of hitting her. But, we'd drilled together as a team for the last few years, day in and day out, so we each knew just what to do. I cut right at an angle, getting off the "X" and out of my partner's line of fire while firing a three-round burst at the target. Meanwhile, Jesse moved offline while firing two blasts of cold iron shot from her Benelli M4.

One of us hit our mark. The target shrieked and collapsed.

Jesse kept her eyes and the muzzle of her shotty trained on the shadowy figure as she slowly advanced toward the center of the cavern. While she moved forward, I took up a position to her rear, sweeping the rest of the cave with my gaze and the barrel of my Glock.

As Jesse approached the target, I backed up, keeping her in my peripheral vision at intervals.

My partner pulled up ten feet short of the target. "Something isn't right."

"Is it dead or not?" I said as I scanned the rest of the cave for more activity.

"I can't tell. It's not moving, that's for sure."

"Is it her?"

Jesse tsked. "If I knew that, would I have stopped?"

"Good point. Put another couple of rounds in it, and see what happens."

My partner jacked two more shells in her shotgun and fired on the figure once more. Instead of hitting the target, the iron buckshot ricocheted right back at us. I hissed as two .32 caliber pellets hit me in the arm and leg. Jesse cursed loudly, indicating that she'd taken the brunt of the blast.

What the hell was that? My first instinct had been to assume she'd hit some sort of magical barrier. Magic was a given in our line of work, and while it gave the enemy the advantage in certain situations, shit happened. No reason to panic. I ignored the burning sensation in my thigh and upper arm and ran to help Jesse.

She turned toward me, and while it looked like she'd been grazed on the temple by at least one pellet, most of them had hit her vest. Eyes wide, blood running down the left side of her face, Jesse looked at me in shock.

"I'm fine—now run!" she screamed as she limped away from the fallen, lifeless figure behind her.

Instead of fleeing, I moved toward her, intending to give her an assist while we retreated and regrouped.

I never got the chance.

Just before she reached me, an invisible force sent her rocketing across the cave. Like a rag doll thrown by an angry child, she slammed into the limestone surface with a sickening crunch. Momentarily stunned, I watched helplessly as Jesse slid down the wall in a bloody, crumpled heap near a cluster of stalagmites.

And that's when a huge, scaly, reptilian creature coalesced in the center of the cave.

THE DRAGON WAS EASILY forty feet from the tip of her nose to the end of her tail. Ruby-red, slitted crocodile eyes, set deep beneath a bony brow on her serpentine head, fixed me with a predatory stare. Her body was a cross between that of a lion and a lizard—powerful and built for speed, but with large, leathery wings draped along her sides. Scales and spiny protrusions lined her back, fading from inky black to deep crimson on her sides, and ending in bright red on her underbelly.

I glanced at where Jesse had fallen in a crumpled heap, and she wasn't moving. Based on the sound her body had made as she hit the cave wall, I suspected that she was badly injured. Time was of the essence, and I desperately needed to get Jesse back to Finnegas. The old man's skill at healing magic was second to none, and if anyone could help her, he could.

First things first—deal with the dragon.

Swishing her spiked tail, Caoránach watched me like a cat as she absently clicked her long, dagger-like claws on the cavern floor.

"Hello, hunter," she hissed in a deep, rich female voice.

Fuck—she's huge.

Finn's intel had been wrong—oh, so wrong. We were supposed to be facing a weak demoness locked inside her humanoid form, not a grown dragon. A succubi-level creature, I could handle alone, but a full-on wyrm? No.

So, my priority was getting us the hell out of here. But, that wasn't going to happen unless I took out the dragon. The only problem was, I didn't have anything handy that could slay her.

Maybe I can't kill her, but I can wound her badly enough to save Jesse.

I holstered my pistol, while angling my body to hide my right hand as I slid it inside my Craneskin Bag. It operated like a bag of holding, the only difference being that my Bag was where Gygax and his gang had gotten the idea in the first place. Frankly, the thing kind of

creeped me out, but it was great for storing surprises—
like the one I'd spring on Caoránach.

"Were you expecting someone...smaller?" the dragon
taunted.

"In fact, I was." I acted as casual as possible while I
stared down a creature that could bite me in two with
one snap of her jaws. "Our sources told us you were
stuck in your human form. Funny how that info could be
so very wrong—almost like we were fed bad intel."

She chuckled, a sound so deep I felt the bass in my
chest. "When you deal with fae creatures, you should
expect misdirection. But, enough of this. You've killed
an ample number of my subjects, and it's time I dealt
with you pesky infants, once and for all."

Caoránach drew herself up to her full height,
opening her jaws like a snake ready to strike.

Now.

When the dragon's head came down at me, I side-
stepped and pivoted. Simultaneously, I pulled my spear,
point first, from my Bag. As her huge jaws clamped
down on empty space, I lunged forward and thrust the
spear at her left pupil. The tip of the enchanted weapon
was razor-sharp, so I met only a small amount of resistance as the spearhead pierced the surface of her eye. I
continued the thrust, burying the leaf-shaped blade to
the shaft.

The dragon's eye burst outward, showering me in

the clear vitreous fluid that had filled her eyeball. She roared with pain and anger, jerking her head away so quickly the spear was snatched from my grasp. Before I could dodge out of the way, she swiped her massive front claw across my midsection, gutting me from stem to sternum.

I looked down at what had been my abdomen, only to find that Caoránach had practically disemboweled me. Half my intestines were strung out across the cavern floor, and what remained of my midsection was a wet mess of bloody, shredded tissue. Falling to my knees, I grasped at my innards in a futile attempt to stuff them back inside my body.

"Motherfucker." I stared at the mangled guts I held in my hands. "This did not go the way I planned."

Then, something burst within my stomach cavity, and a flood of hot, red liquid flowed through my hands. My senses were immediately overwhelmed by the metallic smell of my own fluids, combined with the odors of shit and undigested food that leaked from the tattered remains of my bowels. Instantly weakened by massive blood loss, I fell in a limp heap, my innards squishing and splashing around me.

Aorta must've burst. Damn, I did not think I would go out this way.

Too weak to move, I watched Caoránach pull the spear from her eye. With another primal roar, she tossed it away. The edges of the scene before me began to blur, and my heart fluttered, failing within my chest.

Not enough blood left to pump. This is it.

As darkness crept in and my consciousness faded, my last thought was that I'd failed Jesse.

Sorry, Jesse. I'm so very sorry.

Then, my body spasmed. Every muscle contracted at once. Simultaneously, my thoughts became clearer, although I no longer could control my movements. It seemed as though I was having an out-of-body experience, except my point of view stayed right inside my head. It was quite different from movie death scenes, where the POV drifts up to the ceiling as the camera pans down to a lifeless corpse.

Is this what dying is like? You just stay trapped inside your dead body, watching helplessly as it decays away?

Before I could further puzzle over my current situation, a second presence emerged inside my mind. No, not inside my mind: inside *me*. It was almost as if I'd birthed a second personality from the depths of my own identity and ego, except it wasn't me at all.

No, this secondary presence was hostile and feral. It growled at me, then it came to the fore, shoving my own personality out of the way as it stepped front and center into the light. Suddenly, I was a passenger inside my own head, and someone else was piloting the ship.

An inhuman howl of rage boiled up from within my

body, totally and completely independent of my conscious, autonomous control. As that primal roar escaped my lips, my physical form began to change. Even worse, I *saw* myself transform into something new and hideous, through eyes that were no longer my own, from inside a body I no longer controlled...

That's when the real nightmare began.

ONE

Cognoscenti Therapy Associates, Austin, TX—Eighteen Months Before Present Day

I sat across from Dr. Larsen in her office, which was located in a hip, upscale business complex in a newly gentrified area of East Austin, just a few blocks from the downtown district. She looked at me attentively, waiting for me to answer her last question. I did my best to avoid making eye contact. I tried to find a way to begin, but when I opened my mouth I just couldn't find the words. So, Dr. Larsen posed her question again.

"Tell me about the night Jesse died."

"I can't talk about it—it's too painful."

She readjusted her position in her chair, pulling her skirt down slightly to maintain her perfectly coiffed appearance. I glanced up at her, and reflected that she sure didn't look like a Larsen. She was very pretty, with fine Roman features and the kind of olive skin you couldn't get from a tanning bed or spray booth. She had dark, thick hair, lush, but not quite full lips, and the body of a runway model. I noted this all in a sort of detached, clinical manner, because it distracted me from the topic of discussion.

Namely, how I'd murdered the love of my life.

I'd been referred to Dr. Larsen by Finn's assistant Maureen, the girl who ran his import-export business. The business was a cover for what we really did behind the scenes, before Finn became an addict. Anyway, Maureen was a half-kelpie who'd been handling Finn's affairs for several centuries. In the aftermath of what happened at the Caoránach's lair, Maureen had found me a therapist who knew about the world beneath. Dr. Larsen had a Ph.D. in clinical psychology and a master's in psychiatric nursing, and she knew all about the supernatural realm. How, I had no idea, but this was just about the only place it was safe for me to talk about what had really happened that night.

The official story, the one told to our parents, friends, and family to cover up what had actually happened, was that Jesse and I had been camping together at Inks Lake. While I'd been on a run to the store, she'd gotten attacked by a black bear. It was total rubbish, obviously, because there's no way a black bear could do what had been done to Jesse's body. Only a monster could do such a thing. And that monster was sitting right here in Dr. Larsen's office.

Dr. Larsen finished adjusting her skirt and tapped her pen once on her clipboard. "You'll have to talk about it eventually, Colin, in order to process the pain of those memories. Otherwise it's going to eat you alive. You'll end up just another statistic. I believe you have way too much potential to throw away your life at such a young age."

"Potential? You mean for hunting *them*? Let me tell you, that part of my life is over. All it's done is brought misery to me, tragedy and heartache to Jesse's family, and—"

I stopped, because I couldn't say what I'd been about to say next. Dr. Larsen finished my sentence for me. "And it cost you the love of your life."

I nodded and looked off at the wall. My voice was paper thin and nearly inaudible as I replied. "Yes."

"And you still blame yourself." A statement, not a question.

I flew out of the chair and roared at her. "Of course I blame myself! I remember everything—everything! Every moment of madness as the curse kicked in. It was like the real me stepped outside myself, and another me —a darker part of me—took over. I was just a passenger as I watched it all happen. And there was nothing, nothing I could do about it!"

I slumped back down into the chair, feeling defeated and drained just by that simple admission of guilt and shame. "You don't know what it's like living with a monster inside you. Every day I live in constant fear that it'll happen again, and that this time I'll kill someone else I love. And every night I relive those moments in my dreams. I can't sleep, because when I do I have to go through it all again. I can't eat, because I get sick to my stomach every time I think about the feel of her blood on my hands."

I paused and stared down at those hands, which had curled into fists in my lap without my awareness. "I can still feel her neck snapping beneath my fingers, and see the light leaving her eyes. And I can't bear it any longer. I just want it to be over, everything, over and done with."

"But you can't die, can you? You've tried to kill yourself—how many times now?"

I snorted with derision. "Seven, if you include the walk I took off the Frost Building last week."

"And every time, the curse takes over, and you wake up somewhere alive and perfectly healthy."

I nodded and placed my head in my hands. "Yes."

She leaned forward and grabbed my hands, pulling them into hers. "Look at me, Colin."

I looked down at the floor, but she continued squeezing my hands, waiting patiently for me to respond. After a few seconds, I looked up and met her gaze. As I did, I caught just the slightest hint of gold in her unnaturally blue eyes.

"You know, your story is not all that unique in the supernatural world. Many a were-creature has had a similar experience the first time they turned. And, similar to your predicament, many therianthropes have tried to commit suicide in the midst of their grief and self-loathing, only to wake up the next day with one less round in their gun. They find themselves no worse for the wear, physically speaking.

"I want you to know that I've treated dozens of people who have had similar experiences to yours, who faced similar tragedy and loss. I don't say that to diminish your feelings or what you've experienced in the slightest—I am sharing this with you so you know there is hope after such a tragedy. Things will feel just a little less heavy and a little easier to bear as time goes on. While the memories and pain will never completely go away, they'll fade over time. Eventually, you *will* learn to live again."

She squeezed my hands a final time and let them go, and I sank back into the chair and laid my head back against the cushion to look at the ceiling. "That may be true, Dr. Larsen, but I just can't find a good reason to keep on living."

She nodded. "It's absolutely understandable that you should feel this way. And no one, not one soul has the right to blame you for not wanting to go on. But the fact remains that you really have no choice in the matter at this time.

"Now, for someone in your situation, there are only a few motivating factors that would be strong enough to keep a person moving forward through the process of healing and recovery. One of them is to seek redemption."

I tilted my head forward and glanced at her. "And the other?"

She sat back and crossed her legs. "Revenge. And frankly, given the choice between redemption and revenge, I'd strongly advise you to choose the former and not the latter. One way offers forgiveness and healing, while the other will only lead to more violence and suffering.

"Moreover, if you seek revenge you could easily have another episode. As you said earlier, there's no telling what could happen should that occur. So I suggest that you continue to work on the mindfulness exercises I've shown you, that you get involved in a spiritual community somewhere where you can connect with loving, caring people, and that you stay on your medication." She scratched out a few lines on a pad in her lap and tore the top sheet off, handing me a script for a refill of the antidepressants she'd prescribed me.

"Definitely stay on the meds, and call me if you need

someone to talk to. I'm here to help. Now, I want to see you again—same time next week."

I forced myself out of the chair, swaying slightly as I stood up. These sessions always took a lot out of me, and I had low blood sugar from not eating since forever. "Gotcha. Meditation, church, people, meds." I tipped my ball cap at her. "Same time next week."

She stood and walked me to the door, reassuring me with a gentle touch on my shoulder as she held it open. "You will get through the pain, Colin, I assure you. You're strong enough to come out the other side of this functioning and intact."

I tried to smile as I nodded. "Alright, Doc. I'll do what you say."

As I walked out of her office, all I could think about was making a choice between revenge and redemption. To be honest, revenge sounded really, really good to me. But I had enough blood on my hands already, which meant there was no way I'd risk another episode by hunting down the witch who had cursed me. And since I didn't think I deserved redemption, it occurred to me that I was basically screwed, for life.

TWO

Journal Entry—Eight Months and Three Days A.J. ("After Jesse")

    Dr. Larsen said I need to write this stuff down, since I can't seem to talk about it in therapy. She says it's necessary for processing my pain. So, here goes...

    In every great love story, tragedy strikes, so I suppose our story is no different from the rest. When I was just a kid, my dad was killed fighting the war in Afghanistan. Losing my father so young had devastated me, and it didn't help that I was pudgy, shy, and nerdy as all hell, too. I withdrew inside myself, and quickly became the target of some pretty vicious bullying. My saving grace was making friends with a pretty little tomboy by the name of Jesse Callahan, who was also a bit of an outcast. From the day we met, it was us against the world.

Nothing they could do to us mattered, so long as we had each other's backs.

A few years later, we were both introduced to the world beneath our own when a vampire dwarf came looking to chow down on my still-beating heart. As it turned out, I was the last in a long line of male descendants of the great Fionn MacCumhaill, a.k.a. Finn McCool. Sometime in the way distant past, Fionn had defeated this vampire dwarf, the Avartagh, staked him, and buried him upside down so he couldn't escape his grave. Well, two thousand years later a construction crew accidentally dug him up, and after he slaughtered them he tracked Finn's family line to America, where he came after me to exact his revenge.

That's when Finnegas the druid showed up. Uncle Finn, as my family had always known him, had been training the McCool family line to fight supernatural creatures for nearly two millennia. And while he hadn't planned on introducing me to the family tradition for a few more years, his timetable got moved up when the Avartagh took over our town and cast a glamour that made everyone's wildest dreams come true.

Only it was nothing like Napoleon Dynamite. People walked around in a daze, the town was a wreck, and the local economy took a nosedive. If you couldn't see through the glamour, everything looked perfect, but in reality people were living like animals and being hunted *by unseelie fae without anyone being the wiser. It took a "chance" encounter with a leprechaun to open my eyes to what was happening, and after that the first thing I did was free Jesse from the Avartagh's spell. Then, we went after him.*

Long story short, I nearly died killing the thing, and soon after that, Finnegas started training the two of us to become hunters and champions. At the time we both thought it was great. We had a secret lair where the old man trained us in hand-to-hand combat, spellcraft, and all manner of violence and mayhem. And we could see through the glamour that kept humans from noticing the supernatural creatures that existed all around them. It was like living in a J.K. Rowling novel... for a time.

Shit. I have to stop now. I'll write more about it tomorrow. It just hurts too much to keep going today.

-McC

AUSTIN, TX—Present Day

The bloody tooth flew through my window, ricocheted off the wall, and landed on my pillow. I knew that it flew through the window because of the sound it made when it pierced the glass at several hundred feet per second. And I knew it was a tooth, because I turned the light on saw it gleaming on my pillow, just inches from where my head had rested moments before.

How did I know it was a human tooth? Because humans are the only species known to replace their teeth with gold facsimiles. The fae races weren't very fond of having metal anywhere in their bodies, even precious metals that didn't cause them pain. And weres and vampires, well—if they lost a tooth, it'd just grow back after a good night's sleep. Or day's sleep, if it had come from a vampire.

Nope, this was a human tooth, no doubt about it. And while I wanted to pretend it had just been some neighborhood kid with a pellet gun, it fell on me to find out who was tuning this person up, and to stop it before they got seriously hurt. Because while the victim may have been human, whoever was dishing out this beating definitely was *not* human—no human could hit someone hard enough to knock a tooth out and send it flying at several hundred feet per second. Plus, the dogs weren't barking, which told me they were using a glamour to hide themselves from the mundane world.

I sighed and stuck my bare feet in my running shoes, heading out my bedroom door into the warehouse. I paused to kiss my fingers and transfer that kiss to Jesse's photo before leaving my room. Two years after Jesse's death, and I was living in a rented room that held nothing more than a cot, a hot plate, a huge steamer trunk, a meditation mat, and plenty of shelves to hold all my books and my dad's classic punk LPs. It wasn't much, but my mom's cousin let me sleep here in exchange for keeping an eye on his junkyard at night. Since I hadn't been able to hold down a real job, this was the best I could manage without having to move back in with my mom. The room came with use of the public restroom facilities (joy) and access to a garden hose out back, which I'd attached to a makeshift outdoor shower for whenever I needed to bathe.

Truth was, it wasn't all that bad. Whenever I wasn't in class I could help out at the counter or in the yard pulling parts, and I got paid for that work just like any other employee. You couldn't beat the rent, considering that I lived in Austin, Texas, where even cheap apartments were well beyond the means of a struggling college student. And, living just off South Congress gave me ready access to public transportation. Plus I was just a short hike from SoCo, where all the cool kids liked to hang out. So I wasn't about to complain about having a cheap place to live for the next six years or so.

As I exited the warehouse, I saw the dogs pacing back and forth and whining by the gates. Rufus and Roscoe were both the result of a love match between a Doberman and pit bull, and they were up for chewing on pretty much anything that crossed over the fence at night. And while they couldn't see or hear whatever was outside the gates, they knew something was up, so they were both anxious to go outside and bite something. I scratched them both behind the ears and gave them the command to stay. Until I knew what was going on, I didn't want some unseelie nasty eating my uncle's dogs.

That was another benefit to living in a junkyard—none of the fae bothered me inside the fence. That was partially because of all the iron and metal, both in the cars and in the sheet metal fence itself, but also because I'd warded the entire property line against any and all fae. I'd had enough of the fae, and wanted nothing more to do with any of them, except for my friend Sabine. Besides, Sabine was only half-fae. While she'd inherited her mother's magic, she took more after her father than her mom, which was just fine by me.

Hoping I'd be able to catch a few extra zzz's before I had to leave for school, I exited the gate and took a few deep breaths to calm myself so I wouldn't accidentally lose control as I confronted the culprits.

And culprits they were—four, in fact. I spied their diminutive silhouettes as I exited the junkyard and crept along the fence to where they were soccer kicking a prone, lifeless figure viciously and repeatedly. While the dogs couldn't sense or smell them, I knew how to see through a glamour and spy on fae who didn't want to be seen. For years I'd been trained on how to fight every supernatural creature, how to combat their magic, and how to cast wards and cantrips that could turn their powers against them. My teacher had been a powerful druid, the best of the best.

And currently, he was lying on the ground, getting tuned up by a bunch of bloodthirsty, drug-dealing red caps. *Not again.*

"What's going on here, fellas? Just out for an early morning stroll and decided to beat up an old man?"

The red caps kept kicking Finn for a few more seconds, until they realized that I was talking to them. I crossed my arms and leaned up against a light pole as I waited for them to stop beating my former mentor senseless. Oh, I suppose I should've jumped in to save him, but then I'd just have been enabling him, and he'd never learn the consequences of his addictions. And besides, he was immortal or damn near it... and I was currently avoiding violence in all its various forms.

The red caps all turned to look at me at once, and one of them spoke to his pals with a thick New York accent. "Hey, 'dis mundane can see us! No fair!"

Ignoring his comment, I watched them to see what they'd do. While modern culture has turned the red caps into harmless little garden gnomes who sell discount airline tickets and hotel bookings, in truth they were nasty, vile, vicious little sociopaths who killed for fun and dyed their caps with the blood of their victims. Like so many other folk legends and fairy tales, their species was far more dangerous and twisted than the stories made them out to be.

The largest of the four dropped his hand to the hilt of a wicked-looking knife, tucked in the white leather belt that held his polyester pants up. He was about a meter tall, sturdily built, and clean shaven. His hair was slicked back under a dark red trilby, and he wore a rather loud silk shirt and a set of gold chains that would make any East Coast guido jealous. A pair of white patent leather shoes topped off the ensemble.

The rest of his crew were similarly dressed. They smelled of cheap cologne and Brylcreem, and sported clothes that made them look more like eighties Italian gangsters than the living nightmares they were. Each of them had a large butcher knife or cleaver hanging from their waists, and they gave me hard stares as their leader spoke up.

"'Dis ain't no business of yours, pal. We're just having a talk with the old man here about a debt he owes us. I suggest youse back off and find something else of interest, or else you're gonna end up like 'dis guy. Capisce?"

THREE

Journal Entry—Eight Months and Ten Days A.J.

Sorry I haven't written in a while. I needed some time to think about how things went down... and I guess to get the courage to keep telling this story.

Like I was saying, Jesse and I spent a few years living out a fantasy novel. Then, shit got real. Unbeknownst to us, this bitter old hag named Fúamnach showed up behind the scenes, and as it turned out, she had a hard-on for Finnegas. He'd once helped this Celtic deity by the name of Aengus Óg behead her, because she'd driven the love of his life Étaín away with a spell that made her roam the world for seven years. Never mind that Étaín had once been married to Aengus Óg's foster father Midir, who was also his half-brother, or that Midir had been married to Fúamnach before Étaín stole him away from her. Sure, Étaín got around alright, but apparently this chick was hell on wheels in the sack, because these fools chased her halfway around the world and were willing to trick or kill anyone and anything that got in their way.

Well, the thing about supernatural creatures is that the really powerful ones can't truly be killed. Oh, sometimes you can permakill their offspring, but the really strong ones aren't of this world. So you can kill their physical form, usually by beheading them or burning them to ash, but when you do their spirit just travels back beyond the Veil to whatever hell they came from, and then in a few hundred years they're over here again doing all the vicious and cruel shit they did before.

So, this Fúamnach witch returned from the dead and has been harassing Finnegas ever since. And a witch she is, in every sense of the word. She was a sorceress among the Tuatha Dé Danann, these old-school Irish deities who were eventually defeated by mankind and forced underground, and who would later become known as the sidhe —faery folk. All the modern fae are their progeny, which explains why they're evil as hell. Fúamnach was among the worst of their kind, bitter and heartless and a master of eldritch sorcery.

And because Jesse and I were Finn's students, we ended up in her crosshairs, dead to rights.

Meh, I'm getting tired now. Think I'll turn in and pick this back up later.

-McC

P.S. This seems to be helping. It's easier writing about it than it is talking about it.

P.S.S. I can't believe I wrote that. What a shitty choice of words.

AUSTIN, TX—Present Day

I nodded to the dwarf. "I 'capisce' just fine. But what I don't understand is why you boys thought it would be a good idea to bring your bullshit down to my junkyard. Didn't Maeve tell you to stay away from here?"

He hacked snot from the back of his throat and spat at my feet. "No high and mighty faery queen tells the *Fear Dearg* what to do. We call our own shots, don't we boys?" He looked back to his crew. Two of them nodded and mumbled in agreement. The third was eyeing me with suspicion.

That last one leaned forward to give me a closer look. "Um, Rocko? This guy here kinda looks familiar." He rubbed his chin and narrowed his eyes at me. "You a hunter from the Circle or sumthin', punk?"

I let out a long, slow sigh and met him stare for stare. "Keep guessing."

The others, in typical fae fashion, were more than eager to rise to the challenge of a riddle, even one that was more like a Trivial Pursuit question than a true hero stumper. They began blurting out guesses, one after another.

"He's a were!"

"No, a vamp!"

"An exorcist!"

"Naw, he looks like a Circle wizard to me!"

I pursed my lips and nodded. "You're getting warmer…"

After a short pause, the smallest of the four shouted from the back. "A ninja!" he exclaimed.

The others eyed him with scrutiny, and the leader scowled. "A ninja? Sal, you stupid chooch—who in the hell believes in ninjas these days?"

Sal looked hurt as he replied. "I just like ninjas, is all."

Rocko pulled off his trilby and gestured as if to backhand Sal with it, and Sal cringed away. The lead dwarf tsked as he returned his hat to his head, and sighed. "Kids 'dese days, I tell you."

He turned to me and raised his hands questioningly. "What the hell are you, kid? I really want to know before we break a few more of this guy's bones, and crack a few of yours for interrupting us."

I sniffed in through my nose and cleared my throat in my fist, then stretched and cracked my neck as I rolled out my shoulders. "Me? Oh, I'm just the last apprentice the guy you're beating on trained."

Rocko laughed. "Apprentice? This punk?" He kicked Finn again, who softly moaned in response. "He's just a washed up old druid, with nuthin' left in the tank."

Sal's eyes went wide, then he snapped his fingers and tapped Rocko on the shoulder.

"Waddya want, Sal?" Rocko roared in response.

"Um, Rocko—that there is the Junkyard Druid."

I rolled my eyes and growled in frustration. "How many times do I have to tell you fae, I'm *not* a druid? I'm a *rígfénnid*, damn it."

Rocko cocked an eyebrow and laughed. "You, a warrior chieftain? For one, I don't see no warrior band behind you, and second, you don't look like no fighter to me."

I shrugged. "Could be. But my ancestor Fionn MacCumhaill was said to be a fair-haired youth once, as well."

Rocko took a step back. "You the one that the witch Fúamnach cursed?"

I nodded. "The one and only."

At that revelation, Rocko and his crew began bowing and scraping away from me, and Rocko apologized profusely. "Kind druid, I had no idea we was interloping on your territory. Forgive us 'dis transgression, and please allow my boys and I to be on our way so we bother youse no more."

My voice got higher and tighter as I strangled out a reply. "For the love of Pete, stop calling me a druid!"

Rocko cringed and cocked his head. "We do not mean to offend, but from what me and my boys have heard, you bear all the standard marks of druid kind."

"How so?" I growled.

"Do you cast spells?"

I nodded. "Yeah, but—"

"Are you a friend to animals, large and small?"

I shrugged. "Sure, but that doesn't—"

"Do you prefer natural garments to manmade materials?"

"This hemp shirt is merely a fashion choice," I huffed.

"And do you always pick up litter wherever you go, even when it's not yours?"

"Yes, but that's just being a good citizen!"

Rocko, Sal and his other two goons gave each other knowing looks. Sal nodded with conviction. "Yep, he's a druid."

I was starting to lose my cool, which I absolutely could not allow to happen. I counted to ten and took a few deep breaths until I found my inner zen.

"Whatever you want to call me is fine. But it still doesn't change the fact that you're beating up my mentor, and in front of *my* junkyard."

The red caps all took a knee, and Sal actually prostrated himself on the ground. Rocko looked up at me as he removed his hat and placed it over his black little heart. "As I said previously, we have no excuse for our actions, and 'derefore we are forced to beg your mercy."

Sal whispered behind his hand to another of Rocko's crew. "Yeah, cuz' I don't want to get ripped limb from limb by no cursed druid—I mean, how am I going to feed Sal junior if I got no arms and legs?"

The other dwarf gasped in exasperation and elbowed Sal hard in the ribs. "Ixnay on the uid-dray, you mook!" he whispered in reply.

I chose to ignore the exchange, and decided they needed to leave before something bad happened. "Fine, you can go. But first you have to pay to replace the tooth."

Rocko looked confused. "What tewt?"

"The tooth you knocked out." I pointed at Finn on the ground, who was now struggling to get up. "He's going to need dental work, and I'm not paying for it."

Sal looked panicked as he stood up and rummaged through his pockets. "Here, take this, it's all I got!" He threw two wads of bills on the sidewalk, where Finn began snatching at them drunkenly.

Rocko glared at the other two red caps, who nodded and mumbled their acquiescence as they likewise dropped wads of cash on the ground. Rocko turned back to me, head bowed. "Now, may we leave wit-out fear of violence or retribution?"

I paused and took a deep breath. "I suppose. But if I catch you back here—"

Rocko cut me off. "You don't gotta worry 'bout that. We won't be bothering youse again. Right boys?" His crew mumbled their agreement.

I squatted to snag the bulk of the cash they'd dropped, before Finn could get his grubby hands on it and spend it on smack; dental work was expensive. As they backed away, I spared them a final glance. "Fine, get out of here before I change my mind."

The dwarves beat feet and disappeared into a 70s model Cadillac parked halfway down the block. After I felt certain they had gone, I got Finn to his feet and helped him to the gate. He smelled of piss, booze, and stale sweat, as well as fresh blood. Once through the gate, I propped him against the fence while I shut and locked it. The dogs sniffed at Finn and licked his hands. Animals loved that guy, especially dogs, who didn't hold grudges and didn't care how screwed up a human was. They'd ignore your faults and love you just the same.

Me? I didn't share that trait.

"You didn't have to do that, you know. I can look after myself just fine," the old man said as I slung his arm over my shoulder and walked him toward the warehouse.

"You're welcome," I replied archly. I noted that he barely weighed as much as my mom, who had always been bird thin. He hardly had any meat on his arm, and I could feel his ribs through his bloody shirt.

"You need to eat more, old man. You can't live off skag and booze forever, you know."

He snorted. "Hell if I can't." Finn stabbed a thumb in his chest. "That's my curse, boy—to live another thousand years with the consequences of all my sins."

I rolled my eyes. "You're a pagan, you don't believe in sin."

"Hah!" he countered. "Who do you think invented the concept, long before the first missionaries set foot on my fair isle? Just because we didn't worship the Christian deity, it doesn't mean we didn't have morals."

"I realize that, Finn—just forget I said anything." As we entered the restroom, I kicked the toilet lid down and helped him take a seat so I could wash him up. Most of his bruises and cuts would be healed by this evening, and any broken bones would heal up within a day or two. The old man was tough, and centuries of magic use had granted him a hardiness and limited immortality that many humans would envy.

But he was right; it was more a curse than a blessing. No one should have to live as long as he had, and bear the weight of seeing so many people you loved die—whether to disease, old age, or violence. Still, after thousands of years, you'd think he'd have developed better coping mechanisms.

I grabbed an old hand towel, wetted it in the sink, and gently wiped the blood from his face and hands. "I loved her too, you know. And if anyone should feel guilt or remorse for what happened to Jesse, it's me. I'm the one who killed her."

He slammed a fist against the wall so hard, I heard a bone crack. "Damn it, boy, how many times do I have to tell you that it wasn't you who killed her, but the *ríastrad*? If I hadn't crossed that evil old crone so many years ago, she might never have cursed you in the first place."

I calmly continued wiping down his badly battered face. "I've told you before, I know what I'm doing when I'm under the curse. And the part of me that takes over? It *likes* the killing and the destruction. I'm the only one to blame, and that's a sin I'll carry to my grave."

"Aye, boy, but your sins are not your own. That blood is on my hands, and I'll atone for it as I see fit."

I tossed the rag in the sink. It dripped watered-down blood that traced pinkish tracks into the rust-stained porcelain. "Fine, keep punishing yourself by numbing the pain with a needle. See if I care."

I turned to leave, but his bony fingers latched onto my hand to stop me. The old man's eyes filled with tears as he looked up at me. "Will you ever forgive me?"

"There's nothing to forgive," I lied. "Now go get some sleep."

I reflected on the current nature of our relationship as I trudged back to my room. Finn was my mentor, and I loved him, but I could never forgive him for putting Jesse and I in that old witch's crosshairs. And while he had to live with the consequences of his actions, I was the one who truly had Jesse's blood on my hands.

That was my cross to bear, damn it. And no amount of Finn's self-loathing behavior would change that fact.

FOUR

Journal Entry—Eight Months, Twelve Days A.J.

So, Fúamnach. Ugh. Alright, let's talk evil bitches.

After centuries of being foiled by Finnegas' magic, which basically cancelled hers out, Fúamnach decided that the best way to get at Finn this time around was to curse his top student, that being yours truly. And she hit me with a whammy, that's for sure. That witch saddled me with the curse of Cú Chulainn, which if you know anything about Irish mythology is a real bitch of a curse. Cú Chulainn was probably the greatest hero of Irish legend, but he was also one screwed up dude. When he got really mad, he'd go into a berserker rage and killed everyone and everything around him, friend or foe. To be honest Cú Chulainn was a bit of a sociopath, and he was known to be the type to stab first and talk later. The guy was more or less a mass murderer, even without going into a berserker rage.

Character flaws of Cú Chulainn aside, that's the curse that Fúamnach laid on me, unbeknownst to any of us. And when we ended up facing the dragon Caoránach, the mother of all demons (another enemy that was passed down to me from my ancestor Fionn MacCumhaill), in the heat of battle the curse was triggered and I laid waste to everything and everyone around me.

Did I kill the dragon? Sure, with my bare hands, apparently. But I also killed a bunch of innocent people, including my best friend and love of my life, Jesse.

Damn it, I can't do this right now. I'll come back to it later.

-McC

AUSTIN, Texas—Present Day

The next morning, I got up early to do some work around the junkyard. I mostly worked in trade for room and board, and part of that involved letting the boss know which vehicles were good candidates to flip, and which were better off as inventory. It was really supposed to be Finn's job, but lately he'd been too messed up to bother, which meant I had to cover for him. I slipped on my coveralls, pulled on a pair of work boots, and headed out into the yard with Rufus and Roscoe on my heels.

Most small animals were afraid of me, but not the dogs. Finn said it was because predators recognized an alpha when they saw one. Apparently, the dogs sensed that "other" side of me, and respected its presence. The flip side of that was everything in the animal kingdom that might be considered prey fled from me on sight. Frightening squirrels, moles, and pigeons hadn't exactly been on my list of career goals when I signed up to be druid-trained, but at least it kept the mice and rats out of the warehouse.

The yard smelled like brake fluid, freshly mown grass, and motor oil, which meant we'd just gotten a delivery of wrecked vehicles in from the auction house. Most were cars and trucks that had been totaled by the last owner's insurance company, who sold them to body shops, used car lots, and junkyards to be salvaged or restored and sold at a profit. Other cars had no apparent damage, but had mechanical or electrical problems that were deemed too difficult or expensive to repair. That's where I came in, because lost causes were my *specialty*.

We avoided trying to salvage totaled cars, because no matter how much work you did to them they'd never drive the same again, and we weren't in the business of ripping people off. But the lost cause cars were often only lacking someone who could diagnose the problem and make the repairs. Cars could be tricky to figure out sometimes, and newer cars even trickier, due to all their electronics. But many times it was something as simple as a frayed wire causing a short, or a bad part missed by the mechanic. Other times it could be something expensive like a bad engine control unit or burned out clutch. My job was to lay hands on the vehicles that came in and use my magic to figure out what was wrong... and how to fix it.

Sure, living in a junkyard sucked, but I wasn't complaining. Money was hard to come by these days, as I had zero job skills and no work history to speak of, and my one source of income—hunting monsters—was no longer an option. I suppose it was fortunate that my druid training came in handy for things other than killing monsters, since I couldn't really put "apprentice level sorcerer and medieval weapons expert" on a resume. So, in a weird way, the years I'd spent learning druid magic hadn't been wasted after all.

I walked up to the first vehicle and put my hands on the hood, shifting my senses to the magical spectrum and reaching out with my magic to "talk" to the car. Cars didn't have a spirit, per se, but they did have a sort of psychometric energy that could be read if you knew what to look for and how to look. And while a car's onboard computer could spit out a trouble code that let you know which system was malfunctioning, a mechanic might still spend hours tracking down the problem and trying to fix it.

My way was a hell of a lot faster, and cheaper in labor costs too, because all I had to do was let my magic tell me what was broken. The first three cars were a bust, which was a drag, but we'd still make our money back on them eventually in parts sales. But the last one, a 2005 Honda minivan that looked to have been well cared for, turned out to be a winner. The van's only issues were a malfunctioning fuel pump and a short in the wiring harness—two easy, cheap fixes. It'd make a good, reliable vehicle for a family in need. I marked it for repairs and left a note regarding what to fix in grease pen on the windshield.

After I finished with the van, my phone started vibrating to let me know I had a text. Only a few people had my number, so it was either Mom asking when I was coming home to visit, Sabine texting me to see what I was doing later, or Belladonna sexting with me for the umpteenth time. I wasn't eager to deal with Mom or Belladonna at the moment, but if it was Sabine I didn't want her to think I was ignoring her. She was really sensitive about stuff like that, so I took great care to make sure I didn't hurt her feelings.

Sabine was a half-glaistig I'd met one day while leaving Dr. Larsen's office. The day we'd met she'd been wearing a long-sleeve shirt in the middle of summer in

Austin, and I could smell fresh blood on her that carried just the slightest tang of fae. I recognized the signs and knew immediately that she was a cutter, and one of Dr. Larsen's patients.

There's a weird sort of unspoken agreement between therapy patients that you don't make eye contact or chat when you run into another patient on the way in or out of your therapy session. Even so, it was easy for me to recognize another person in pain, so I smiled at her as we passed. In response, she barely lifted her hand in a shy little wave, right before she scurried off into Dr. Larsen's waiting room.

I ran into her a few times after that, and it was always the same. I'd smile and hold the door, and she'd wave shyly before scampering off like a scared mouse. Which I thought was kind of amusing, since she was just about the most stunning female I'd ever laid eyes on since I lost Jesse. It made sense, though; Sabine was wearing a permanent glamour to make her *not* look attractive or noticeable... at all.

In fact, her glamour made her look like a mousy, painfully thin, extremely frumped out college aged girl. She wore birth control glasses, baggy clothes, and sported a wild, frizzy blonde hairdo that did a great job of hiding her face when she stared at the ground—which she did most of the time. Combine that with the see-me-not spell she'd cast on herself, and she was practically invisible.

Of course, I could see right through her glamour, because druid skilz and what-not. And what she looked like under all that magic very nearly took my breath away the first time I saw her. Not only that, but it was readily apparent why she was hiding from the world, and what made her hate herself so much.

As it so happened, Sabine had been born with all the right equipment. A bit too much of it, in fact. To put it bluntly, Sabine had rather large breasts. And knowing what I knew about middle school and high school boys, I was certain that she had been harassed mercilessly from the time she began to develop as a woman. Having been cruelly teased throughout the latter part of grade school and all through middle school for having moobs, I could relate to her pain (I could still hear the kids in the locker room chanting "Colin McBoobs." Not cool).

Moreover, if you know anything about glaistigs, you know that they are not naturally top-heavy. Your average glaistig, like most fae, will lean more toward the tall, nimble, Scandinavian model-looking type. Obviously, the poor girl had inherited her bra size from the human side of the family. So, Sabine was teased for her looks both among humans and by her mother's kind as well.

Naturally, I made it my mission to become her

friend. One underdog to another, I started rooting for her from the moment we met. It took me a while, because she was damned skittish, but finally I coaxed her into joining me for coffee at La Crème. Since I had a supernatural ability to look women in the eye no matter what they looked like or how low their neckline is—a skill drilled into me by my very traditional Irish mother and refined by the very tough and traditionally feminist love of my life—I was able to keep up the charade that I couldn't see through her glamour for the next several weeks.

By which time, I might add, we'd become fast friends. I found her to be smart, charming, and absolutely hilarious. Sabine had a rapier wit, and when she chose to reveal it she could cut even the most arrogant and self-important asshole down to size. At first she was angry with me for not telling her that I was immune to her glamour, but then she realized that I didn't care what she looked like one bit. I liked her for who she was, not what she was, and I think that realization kept her from bolting for the door when she found me out.

So, Sabine became my supernatural confidante, one of the few people in my life I could talk to about supernatural matters without being asked if I was off my meds. Mom had never been clued in, so I couldn't talk to her, and I wasn't really on speaking terms with Finn. All Belladonna ever wanted to do was speak in double-entendres, with the occasional interlude to describe her latest assignment, so no dice there. Anyway, for the most part I tried to stay away from Bells, not just because I was trying to stay out of supernatural affairs, but also because I just wasn't ready for a relationship of any kind.

That was the other benefit to having a bestie who was actually a drop-dead gorgeous fae. Belladonna, who could also see through Sabine's glamour, just assumed we were sleeping together and that the reverse glamour was my idea as a jealous boyfriend—and for my part I did nothing to dissuade her from that assumption. And Belladonna, while being a very liberated, modern woman, was nothing if not honorable. So, while she respected the boundaries of my supposed relationship with Sabine, I got a break from Belladonna's full court press. All-in-all, it was a rather neat arrangement. And Sabine, being Sabine, was absolutely clueless regarding the whole deal.

Yeah, it was messed up. But then again, so was my life.

SURE ENOUGH, the text was from Sabine.

1st day of class. Don't b 18.

According to my phone, I still had time to stop by La Crème on the way. It was too late to head out back to shower, because I could already hear the early crew moving around in the warehouse. I grabbed my shaving kit and ducked into the bathroom, settling for a sponge bath, a quick shave, and a rather thorough round of dental hygiene. I put on a pair of nearly clean jeans, a fresh t-shirt, my leather jacket, and some kicks. Finally, I grabbed my Craneskin Bag out of the only warded space in the room, my foot locker, and slung it over my shoulder before heading out.

Before leaving my room, I picked up Jesse's photo from the shelf by the door and kissed it lightly. "First day of school, babe. Wish me luck."

As I headed out to the parking lot to hop on my vintage, slightly beat up Vespa, my mom's cousin Ed yelled at me from the office. Ed owned the place, and he was the reason I wasn't living in my mom's basement at the moment. I jogged up to the door to see what he wanted.

Ed sat behind his desk, as usual. He was a rather rotund man, balding, with a mustache that looked like a fuzzy caterpillar had taken up residence on his upper lip. A nearly constant pissed off demeanor served as his happy mode. You only had to worry about Ed when he stopped yelling and screaming at people.

"Hey, Colin, anything happen last night? The dogs were acting weird when I came in, and there was some blood on the floor in the warehouse."

I shook my head. "Nothing major, Ed. Finn got

messed up again, and fell and cut himself coming over the fence. I cleaned him up in the bathroom and got him settled into his van. No biggie."

As evidence of how big-hearted Ed actually was, he put up with letting Finn sleep in a junked van in the back of the yard. Truth was, Finn could be handy with getting old cars to run, when he wasn't messed up on smack. So Ed let him stay, in exchange for helping us flip used cars. But Ed also knew about Finn's habits, and chose to look the other way so long as he didn't bring any drugs on the premises.

Ed frowned and shook his head. "I know he's related to you by your dad and all, but that old man's going to get himself killed one of these days. You ought to see about getting him some help, before—you know."

"I know. Believe me, I know. But he's just not ready to get cleaned up yet. I'll keep trying, Ed—I owe him that."

Ed waved with the back of his hand and sighed through his nose. "Damned shame. He's good with a wrench, and I could use him around here full-time if he was clean. Speaking of which—"

He pulled an envelope from the desk and tossed it to me frisbee-style. I snatched it out of the air. "That's pay for this period."

"Ed, it's not payday yet."

He waved again and tried to look like a hard-ass.

"Yeah, but I know you got school starting, and you need books and stuff. So I figured I'd give you an advance." Then, with a stern look, he pointed a single fat finger at me. "But don't think you aren't going to work it off this week."

It went without saying. "Thanks, Ed. Speaking of which, the Odyssey is the only one from the latest bunch that's worth wrenching on—the rest are all going to be parts cars."

"Alright, I'll let the crew know. Now, get out of here and go learn something, so you don't have to work for me for the rest of your life."

He gave me a dismissive wave and turned his attention to his computer monitor. I smiled and tucked the check into my back pocket, and headed off to get some coffee before class.

FIVE

Journal Entry—Eight Months, Fourteen Days A.J.
It's Valentine's Day. God, I miss her so much.
-McC

AUSTIN, Texas—Present Day

My friend Luther's coffee shop was a kind of frou-frou, upscale cafe located right at the edge of SoCo and downtown, where the local jet-setting movers and shakers who inhabited the expensive downtown district liked to slum it up with the people who made up the true heart of Austin; the hippies, artists, musicians, and hipsters who did a damned fine job of keeping Austin weird.

La Crème was a favorite hangout for grad students who lived off-campus, for office workers who needed a few minutes away from their daily bustle, for decision-makers and power-brokers who tried to look chic while they closed on multi-million dollar deals, and for all the struggling writers, musicians, and artists who could barely afford to live in Austin proper anymore because of the property tax hikes the wealthy people in Austin voted for each election cycle.

Oh, and it was a favorite hangout for folks who were read in on the world beneath. I knew I was supposed to be staying away from that sort of thing. But Luther poured a mean cold-brew and he always saved me a cup, even when they sold out. Plus, Luther was a vampire, and the de facto leader of the vampires in Austin. He was also a fixture in the local LGBTQ community, so La Crème was pretty much a place where everyone was welcome to hang out.

Luther was a very old vampire, and like a lot of older vamps he might have swung either way, depending on which century it was. When you're nearly immortal you tend to try new things, which meant a lot of older vamps were pretty accepting of so-called alternate lifestyles. And, like most of vampire society in Austin, Luther had become heavily involved in the gay and lesbian community in the last several decades.

And just why would a three-hundred-year-old vampire choose to blend in among the LGBTQ community? Well, to put it in Luther's words, "Honey, nobody screws with the Velvet Mafia. No one. I'm a gay black man, and a vampire. That gets me a lot of enemies. But for the first time in history I can live a public life, and not have to worry about being singled out for being gay or found out for being a vamp. So hooray for strength in numbers."

When I'd first heard him say that, I informed him that he was showing his age, because no one called it "The Velvet Mafia" anymore—and that there was no such thing as the "gay mafia," anyway. Luther disagreed.

"It's everywhere now, sugar. The gay community is out of the closet and marching down Main Street. And they protect their own. What better community and culture for my kind to hide in, and in plain sight, than among a group of people who never question the way anyone talks, or dresses, or who they keep company with, or why they're never seen outdoors in the daytime? Most queers are natural night owls and party animals anyway. So we vampires fit right in, and no one pays us any mind at all."

I had to admit, the overall strategy of hiding in plain sight that the vampire community had adopted was brilliant beyond belief. And, I couldn't fault them for just wanting to be left alone. Besides, it worked. Now that they had a good thing going they policed their own, which cut down considerably on vamps killing humans. Unlike their more barbaric Nosferatu brethren, higher order vamps could control their prey drive. Most of them either fed via private blood banks, or they made arrangements with their human lovers to feed. All of this helped maintain the uneasy truce they kept with the Cold Iron Circle, which was what passed for the supernatural police in these parts.

Not only was Luther solid for a good cup of joe, he was also a damned good guy to have in your corner when you needed it. As an important figure in the local vamp community, he more or less kept the Circle off my case. Last year, I'd helped him with a nosferatu problem that was bringing a little too much heat on the vamps, and since then he'd always had my back.

Soon after I'd helped him get rid of the nos', the harassment I'd been getting from the Circle stopped, and suddenly I didn't have to look over my shoulder anymore. For decades, the vamp community had kept an uneasy peace with the Circle, and both sides preferred to keep it that way. So when I came under Luther's protection, that was that. They still saw me as a major threat, but since there hadn't been another "incident," they'd mostly backed off and left me alone. Which was fine by me. But, it didn't mean that I didn't still occasionally get harassed by those assholes, either.

So, Luther and I were cooler than cool. That was, so long as none of his vampires stepped over the line.

I parked my Vespa in my usual spot—right up on the

sidewalk—and walked inside La Crème, nodding to Luther as I entered. When he saw me, he gave me a funny look and kind of tilted his head toward the back room. Me being the clueless person I was, who never picked up on social cues and subtlety, simply gave him a puzzled look back and walked up to the counter to order.

"I'll have my usual, Luther."

He rolled his eyes and sighed, right about the time I heard Belladonna's whiskey voice coming from the back room.

"Well, look at this tall drink of water who just walked in. Hello, loverboy."

Dressed in her usual tight leather pants, clingy tank top, biker jacket, and high-heeled biker boots, Belladonna was vampier than any of Luther's friends by far. Her dark, luscious hair somehow managed to pick up a breeze as she sashayed up to me (I suspected a cantrip at play). She smiled seductively as she leaned in and tugged at the lapel of my coat with a single, perfectly manicured finger. How she managed to kill all those monsters without ever breaking a nail was beyond me, but her French manicure was flawless.

"Since you're still avoiding me, McCool, then I take it you're also still seeing that half-fae cow, Sabine?"

I leaned back and plucked her hand from my collar. "Now now, be nice, Belladonna. Sabine is a sweet girl, and she's very sensitive about her looks."

"Oh, honey, I know she's not around. And if she was, I'd never step on her toes anyway. I may be forward, but I do respect certain boundaries." She tsked and catwalked around me, trailing a finger across my body as she stalked her prey.

"And besides, you've never shown any interest in me at all. Why, if I didn't know any better, I'd think you have a thing for Luther here." Belladonna pouted and stuck out her lower lip as she completed her circuit, ending it standing uncomfortably close to me once more.

Luther stifled a laugh at her last remark, since he knew I wasn't bi-curious in the slightest. Even so, he held his tongue as he prepared my cold brew behind the counter. Luther knew that I was attracted to Belladonna —very much so, in fact—but that I was old-fashioned in a way that only a traditional Protestant upbringing and a very limited experience with women can produce. Not that I held Belladonna's sexual freedom against her; far from it, in fact. I actually envied her ability to let her inner animal loose, as it were.

No, it was just that I had experienced the kind of love that most people only dream about, and quite frankly I wasn't about to try to replace it with 3:00 a.m. booty calls and a polyamorous sleeping arrangement. Especially not when I had feelings for her; confused feelings, but feelings nonetheless. Belladonna had helped me through some rough times, and she'd taken a lot of shit from the Circle for being my friend. She was a better hunter than most, but had been passed over again and again for leadership positions because of her refusal to end our friendship. I felt like I owed her more than just being a casual hook-up.

Like I said, call me old-fashioned.

But it didn't mean that I wasn't tempted. Belladonna might have earned a bit of a reputation for being fast, but the mileage didn't show on her in the slightest. And for an introverted person like myself, the absolute flattery of having a woman like that come onto you was almost overwhelming. Almost. But I'd long ago decided that it was probably best we remain friends.

C'est l'amour.

I decided to play it cool. "Belladonna, you are and always will be one of my dearest friends. But right now, I am fully committed to someone else." *My dead ex, in fact.* "And the timing just isn't right for us. So, please— respect my wishes. Let's not screw up our friendship with cheap, meaningless sex."

She smiled a wicked smile that somehow morphed into a sultry little moue of disappointment. *Damn*, but that woman knew how to turn it on.

"Oh, it wouldn't be meaningless, I can assure you of that," she said. "You'd be unpacking the experience for months after it happened, and pondering the many personal realizations uncovered by achieving that level of ecstasy—perhaps for *years* to come." She released the subtle pout of her lips ever so slightly, then stepped back just enough to signal a temporary detente. "But I suppose it can wait for another time."

I smiled and barely withheld a relieved sigh. "Thanks. Now, I know you're never up this early unless you pulled an all-nighter or you need an assist on a tough gig. What's up?"

She was all business now, and switched gears without missing a beat. "Might be nothing, but we've been investigating some murders that look suspiciously like 'thropes are involved. I might need some help looking into it, if another body pops up tonight."

"Hmmm... Crowley can't do it?"

Crowley was supposed to be her partner, a Circle wizard on the fast track to management before he'd hit thirty. The Circle always paired a hunter and a wizard, knowing that each partner's strengths complemented the other. Most weren't like me, druid-trained in both magic and physical combat. Of course, I was limited to the basics of magic—mostly wards and cantrips that were good for investigative work and B&E, but not much else. Still, it did the trick.

She scowled at the mention of Crowley. "No, that prick is still pissed that I broke it off with him. I told him that if we slept together it was just going to be a way to pass the time on stakeouts, but he had to go and fall in love with me. The jackass."

Luther chimed in as he set my drink down on the counter. "Tell me about it. Some men just don't know what's good for them." He flashed me an accusatory look as he wiped down the counter.

She glanced over at Luther and gave him a nod. "You got that right. See, Luther here has his priorities straight. You sure you don't swing hetero every now and again, babe?"

He looked her up and down and gave his best Mae West grin. "Not in the last hundred years or so, but in your case I might be tempted, sweet thing."

That seemed to lift her spirits, and when she smiled it lit up the room. "I'll take that as a compliment, Luther. Thank you."

Then she leaned in and surprised me with a quick peck on the cheek, before I even knew what was happening. Damn, but she was quick. Her fingers lightly dragged across my chest as she turned to walk away.

"Keep your phone on tonight, Colin. If you hear from me, it won't be for a booty call." Luther and I both watched her departure as she walked out the back door, her perfect figure and graceful gait garnering stares from male and female patrons alike.

Luther shook his head and rolled his eyes. "Mmm-mmm, but that woman knows how to make an exit.

Almost makes me want to go straight for a while, to explore the joys and wonders of the Kama Sutra with her for a decade or two."

He looked at me and chuckled. "You better have your health insurance paid up, if you ever decide to take her up on that standing offer."

I tilted my head and arched an eyebrow. "I might, if I thought the arrangement would be exclusive."

Luther pursed his lips and nodded. "Ever tell her that?"

"Nope."

"Uh-huh. So how you know how it's gonna be if you don't?"

I shrugged. "You got me there. Maybe I'm just afraid of being hurt."

"Or hurting someone else." His eyes softened and he gave me a knowing smile. "Coffee's on me today, kid. Don't be late for class."

SIX

Journal Entry—Eight Months, Nineteen Days A.J.

At first, I didn't remember any of it, at least not the parts that happened after the curse took over. I think my mind blocked it out initially, in the days after Jesse died. The last thing I do remember is getting the shit kicked out of us by that dragon. She was supposed to have been too weak to shift into her dragon form, having just come back from the dead and all. But she did, and once that happened we were royally screwed.

In retrospect, Finnegas pushed us into that situation way too soon, and long before we were ready to face such a powerful creature. But the Caoránach was trying to open a doorway to hell to free her children—and cause the end of the world as we know it and all that jazz—so of course it fell on us to stop her.

Which brings me to the reason why I hate Finnegas so much. See, we weren't the only people qualified to fight that battle—not by a long shot, in fact. In every age, champions, plural, are born to fight the forces of evil. I know, it's cliché as hell, but it's a fact. And there aren't just a few of us born, because if that was the case then we'd soon be overwhelmed... because there are an ass-ton of monsters out there lurking in the shadows.

It's not like there's a glut of champions running around, but there are a lot. Roughly one in a thousand children are born with the gift. Most of them live their lives never knowing they're genetically designed to kick monster ass and take supernatural names. But maybe one in a hundred have a chance run-in with a supernatural baddie, and that awakens their powers. Those who survive their initial encounter with the paranormal eventually become hunters, warriors, wizards, druids, and the like—whatever path their cultural heritage sets them on.

And if that sounds crazy, then this will really blow your mind. Most famous heroes out of history were actually champions pushing back against the F.o.E., the forces of evil. Geronimo, William Wallace, Davy Crockett, Billy the Kid, Constantine, Wong Fei Hung... they were all champions, and all of them killed their fair share of supernatural creatures.

Also, a lot of the major events in history were cover-ups for the eternal war. The French Revolution? That was really about rampant vampirism among the French royalty... which explains all the beheadings, if you think about it. The Napoleonic Wars? That was a further effort to purge Europe from supernatural creatures completely. You think Manifest Destiny was about land and resources? Well, it sort of was, but it was really about the European supernatural powers that be trying to stamp out the supernatural powers in the New World, so they could steal their power for themselves. I could go on and on, but you get the point.

Anyway, my point is that there was really no good reason for us to be in that cave fighting a dragon. Finn should've found a more experienced team to handle it, or he should've been there himself.

Aw hell... I'm too pissed right now to keep writing. Maybe I'll talk about it more tomorrow.

-McC

AUSTIN, Texas—Present Day

I thanked Luther for the free coffee, and then remembered I had never asked Belladonna where those murders had happened. I figured with it being the first day of school and all, I might want to get a head start on helping her before my professors decided to load on the homework. I ran out the back door after her, only to see the tail lights of her Harley driving off into the distance.

I chased her halfheartedly, but decided it wasn't worth the effort. Instead, I sent her a text as I took a shortcut through the alley next to La Crème so I could hop on my scooter and head to class.

As I was finishing my text to Belladonna, I got blindsided and pinned to the alley wall. Not by anything physical; this was a magical attack. My phone went flying along with my coffee, and I watched in slow motion as the lid flew off my cold brew, spilling the contents on the asphalt below.

"Noooooooo!" I screamed as I watched my phone hit the pavement next to my cup. A cracked screen was no big deal. I mean, I was druid-trained for Pete's sake, so repairing a cracked glass pane was no biggie. But the coffee was the real loss, because I'd witnessed Luther pouring the last dregs of cold brew from the decanter just moments before.

I looked up from the crime scene to see who'd attacked me, but I already had a good idea who it might be. And, of course, who should come strolling out of the shadows but Crowley himself. If I'd been paying attention, I would've noticed the unnaturally dark area halfway down the alley, which could only have been caused by a shadow magic user's concealment spell. Crowley's magic manipulated shadows and light and bent them to his will; in fact, the spell that held me pinned to the alley wall was made up of solidified shadow. Neat trick, that.

He smirked as he strutted up to me, all six feet plus of his slightly awkward and gangly self. Crowley looked a lot like a young Jeff Goldblum, all long limbs and elbows, but good looking in an exotic, 'I'm here to clean your pool and rub sunscreen on your back' sort of way. As usual, he wore a long, dark trench coat, a black silk shirt unbuttoned halfway down his chest to reveal the pentagram medallion he always wore, dark slacks, and a damned fine looking pair of Italian leather dress shoes. His dark curly hair surrounded the lean Mediterranean landscape of his face like a halo of liquid shadow, and flashes of light danced in his eyes as he sauntered over.

I had to hand it to the guy; he had swagger.

He grinned mirthlessly as he looked me up and down. "Well now, look what I've caught in my web of shadows. A mentally defective, witch-cursed druid who thinks he can get away with murder."

I struggled against the spell, but no dice. I had to admit, the guy was good and he'd gotten the jump on me. If I'd been expecting it, I might have released a counter-spell to loosen the bonds so I could struggle free. But currently, I was at his mercy. I did my best to remain calm as spoke my displeasure.

"Crowley, I don't have time for your petty bullshit

today. I'm going to be late for class. Let me down and I'll forget this ever happened."

He tsked and stepped into bad breath range, patting me on the cheek. "You'll forget this ever happened, eh? Like you forgot how you killed all those people in Kingsland? You dismembered over a dozen people, McCool. And one of them was your partner! You think you can just sweep that under the rug and make it go away?"

I hung my head, partially in shame and remorse for what I'd done, and partially because looking at Crowley was making my head hurt. "No, Crowley, I don't. I have to live with it every single day. But you and I both know it was the curse that did it, not me. I was merely the vessel that channeled Fúamnach's evil magic."

At that name, I saw his fingers curl into fists. *Interesting.* I tucked that info away and pretended that I hadn't noticed his reaction.

"Ah yes, the witch who was killed thousands of years ago, beheaded by a long dead god, who no one has seen in over two thousand years. Right."

I sighed. "Look, we can play this game all day. But in the end, you know that if you mess with me you'll start a war between the vampires and the Cold Iron Circle that'll tear this city apart. And you and I both know that your bosses in the Circle would have your ass in a sling if your little vendetta against me set off that powder keg."

His eyes narrowed and he gave me a stare that could

have curdled milk. After a few seconds pause, he snapped his fingers and released the spell. I fell from where he'd been holding me and landed lightly on my feet. Crowley was already walking back into the shadows of the alley.

He glanced over his shoulder at me as he walked away. "You're a menace, McCool—a ticking time bomb in the middle of over a million people. Last time the curse took over, it was out in the middle of nowhere. Next time it's going to be a disaster of epic proportions. I intend to take you out before that happens."

I watched him fade away as he vanished into the cloak of shadows that curled around him. It was a cool trick, but I suspected he was still present and hidden in the dark recesses of the alley. A newb would think he had teleported, which was what he'd intended me to think—but teleportation spells were damned near impossible to do.

Like I said, he had style.

After he'd disappeared from view, I pulled my hand out of my Craneskin Bag, releasing the enchanted spear I'd had ready in case things had escalated. Pretending that his accusations hadn't affected me, I strolled through the alley and into the bright fall sunshine as if nothing had happened.

But the truth was, that little run-in had cast a dark shadow over what should have been a day of celebration.

As I hopped on my scooter and rode off to class, I couldn't help but dwell on fears that I'd worked hard to overcome. Crowley was right. I *was* a ticking time bomb. And until I found a way to remove Fúamnach's curse, I'd never truly be free from the paralyzing possibility that I might lose control and kill again.

SEVEN

Journal Entry—Eight Months Twenty-One Days A.J.

So yeah, Finnegas could have found any number of people who had the juice to take on the Caoránach, but instead he pushed us into doing it. Why... to prove a point? I don't know. All I know is that his hubris led to my curse and the death of the woman I loved, and by my own hand.

Which is why I've washed my hands of the whole lot of it. Magic, fighting the forces of evil, dealing with the fae, everything. My plan is to finish my undergrad, apply to grad school, and live out my life in complete anonymity, far, far away from all the madness of the world beneath our own.

The only problem with my plan is, the supernatural world won't leave me alone. Try as I might, I can't seem to keep it out of my business. But the good news is that they can't force me to be part of their mess, right? And no matter how hard that world pushes, I won't budge. Nope, it's the mundane life for me, from here on out.

-McC

P.S. Screw Finn. I hope he dies in a crack house somewhere.

P.S.S. I really don't, but I wish I was capable of that much hate. It might feel better than being so conflicted about the old man.

AUSTIN, Texas—Present Day

The run in with Crowley had definitely shaken me up, but I wasn't going to let it ruin my day. It had taken me months to get to the point where I could tackle starting school, and I wasn't going to let anything take the joy of this milestone away from me. As I cruised up Guadalupe and onto campus, I reflected on all the struggle and pain that had brought me to this point.

Yes, I was a murderer. But I was also innocent, since it hadn't been me who'd killed all those people, but Fúamnach's evil magic working *through* me. And as tragic as it all was, ultimately it wasn't my fault. There was no way I could've stopped those events from occurring, because I had no idea at the time that I'd been cursed.

But I do know now. I pulled into a parking spot next

to a brand new Kawasaki KLR-650. I used the bike as a distraction from my current train of thought, and wondered if I could save up enough money for down payment on a 250. Maybe Luther would give me a part-time gig at the coffee shop to supplement the money I made working for Ed.

I could start hunting monsters for cash again. Yeah, when pigs flew. That'd put me squarely back into the exact situations I was trying to avoid. Best that I just put all thought of buying a sweet dual-sport bike out of my mind, and focus on school for the next eight years or so. Because the safe money was on a career in the mental health fields. It didn't pay that great, but it didn't come with the risk of going on a homicidal killing spree, either.

I gave one last longing look at the bike as I locked my helmet onto my beat up old Vespa and headed into the lecture hall. Since I was enrolled in all general ed courses this year, I'd be attending most of my classes in the famed mass lecture halls on campus. Picture a huge amphitheater filled with hundreds of impressionable freshmen, with a dowdy prof or TA lecturing at the front of the room—that was pretty much what my world was going to be for the next few years.

After wandering around campus for several minutes trying to locate the correct building, I finally found my way to the lecture hall, navigating a sea of incoming freshmen on the way. I looked up into the mass of students taking their seats and saw Sabine waving at me from way up in the nosebleed section.

Great, I thought. *Guess I'll be buying notes online for this class.*

I really couldn't hold it against Sabine, though. That girl was a mess in public, what with her social anxiety disorder and mild case of agoraphobia. She'd come a long way since I'd met her, and in truth we'd leaned on each other a lot in working through our individual issues. It had been her idea to audit the class with me, and although she wasn't officially enrolled at the university, it didn't matter much. No one paid attention to who attended these mass lectures—and besides, nobody ever really noticed Sabine anyway, because of her damned see-me-not spell.

That spell was a bone of contention between us. It made me look like I was talking to myself all the time, and after several awkward situations where people stared at me like I was completely mad, I took to wearing a wireless earpiece whenever I was with her. So, instead of looking like a loon, I just looked like an asshole. Not much of an improvement, but without her see-me-not spell Sabine was a mess in public. It was a small price for me to pay to get her out of the house on a regular basis.

I trudged up the steps and plopped down next to my bestie. "What's up, Speck?" I asked as I sat down next to her. Speck was the dog in *PeeWee Herman's Big Adventure*, a Tim Burton movie we both loved.

She looked up at me and smirked. "Not you, apparently. You're late. Didn't you get my text?"

"Yes, mom, I got your text. And I am definitely not late. Lecture hasn't even started yet."

She twitched her nose and narrowed her eyes at me in mock seriousness. "No back talk, bub. Now hush, the nice man in the suspenders and bow tie is about to start talking."

I stuck my tongue out at her and settled into my seat, pulling my text, a notebook, a pencil, and a foot-long sub out of my Craneskin Bag. The bag was ugly as sin, but it sure was handy to have around. Finn had given it to me as a sort of inheritance on my eighteenth birthday. It was like a bag of holding, only way cooler, because whatever you stuck in there remained in stasis until you pulled it back out. It was great for storing unruly semi-sentient magical items, and sandwiches you didn't want to spoil.

I began unwrapping my sandwich, which resulted in a lot of paper rustling and associated noises. A very uptight-looking girl in glasses three rows in front of us turned around and shushed me. I flipped her off and Sabine snickered.

"Already making friends, I see," she observed sagely.

"What? I haven't had breakfast yet, and that asshole Crowley made me drop my coffee. Sue me, already." I munched on my sandwich as I listened to the lecture. This guy didn't waste any time whatsoever; he was already telling us to flip to page 63 in the text. I leaned over to Sabine.

"Psst... flip my book to page 63 for me." She pursed her lips and sneered at me playfully. "Hey, I have my hands full here with this sandwich. But don't worry, it'll be gone shortly."

Sabine flipped my book open to the proper page. "There, you big baby. Should I wipe your mouth for you as well?"

"That'd be great, thanks." The uptight chick shushed me again. I raised my sandwich to her. "Want some? There's plenty here for everyone."

She didn't seem at all amused. I guessed some people just didn't appreciate quality cold cuts. As I took another bite, Sabine nudged me and nodded to another girl sitting a few seats down from Ms. Pantywad.

"Hey Colin, I'm pretty sure that girl over there thinks you're cute."

I perked up slightly at that. Not that I was looking for a relationship, but I was still not going to blow off a chance to flirt a little. I mean, I needed the practice. Someday I was going to be free from this curse and ready to move on, and I needed to know I had some game when that day came. Besides, knowing that someone new was interested in you was always a real confidence booster.

I looked where she was staring. "Who, that blonde girl?"

Sabine pulled her glasses down the bridge of her nose and squinted at the girl she'd pointed out. "Oh, hell no. Uh-uh, nope. Forget I said anything."

"What, what's wrong? Why should I forget that a very cute blonde was just checking me out?"

She scowled and shook her head. "Because, she's fae, and a bitch besides. Trust me, you want to stay far away from her. She works for Maeve."

Aw hell. *Maeve.* Faery queen over all of Austin, a domain of no small importance in the world of the fae. She was a royal pain in my ass, too. For some reason she'd taken an interest in me since I settled in Austin, and since then she hadn't left me alone. At least once a week I'd get an invite to a royal event or to have tea with her, and every single time I had to tactfully decline in the least offensive way possible.

The last thing I wanted to do was become entangled in the affairs of the fae. For one, you couldn't trust them. Second, wherever the fae went, violence always followed. And third, Maeve was a wolf in cougar's clothing. She might've looked harmless, even friendly... but that was a facade cultivated over the course of centuries, designed to lull you into a false sense of security. And the minute you let your guard down around her, she'd cut your balls off and hold them ransom until she ran you ragged doing her bidding.

I watched the fae girl out of the corner of my eye during the remainder of the lecture. Sure enough, she was keeping an eye on me. After class was dismissed, she approached us while we gathered our things.

Sabine and the girl appraised each other warily as she waited for me to acknowledge her presence. I sized her up in my peripheral vision as I packed my books into my bag. Her bright green eyes, high cheek bones, and button nose made her pretty, if a little too doll-like. Despite being pulled back in a ponytail, her long blonde hair would have put any girl on a shampoo commercial to shame. She was wearing a collared shirt under a skin-tight elbow-length sweater, a flared skirt that hit about mid-thigh, knee socks, and a pair of Jimmy Choos that cost more than my tuition this semester.

Yes, I spent a lot of time on Pinterest.

"Siobhán," Sabine said icily.

"Sabine," she replied. "Love what you've done with that glamour. I can't decide whether you're going for homeless, or criminally insane. But I have to say, that rat's nest on your head tops off the whole look for you."

Sabine cocked a hip and crossed her arms. "Thanks. Nice stripper outfit, by the way," she deadpanned. She made a megaphone with her hands and called out loudly in the general direction of the podium in an impression of a D.J.'s voice.

"Siobhán, calling Siobhán to the center stage! Get those dollar bills ready, boys, because this girl's grinding her way through a pre-law degree, and mama needs a new pair of shoes!"

I actually thought her outfit was in good taste, but then again I was a guy; we thought thong bikinis were in good taste, too.

She scowled at Sabine, who was looking pretty smug after that comeback. I cleared my throat to draw her attention from my friend and addressed her directly.

"Whatever ball, dinner party, or other gastronomic function Maeve has planned, please tell her that I am indisposed and I apologize but I won't be attending."

Siobhán shook her head slightly. "Sorry cutie, but you're not getting off that easily. Maeve said that she requests your presence immediately. Meaning, this is not an invitation, but a command appearance. I suggest that you head straight over, because unlike most older fae, she's not known to be a patient queen."

I happened to look over and stifled a laugh, because Sabine was mimicking her as she spoke. She graced Sabine with a haughty glance and then turned to address me again.

"I suggest that you be on your best behavior. Something has her all worked up, and the last time I saw her like this she turned the gardener into a toad. The poor guy lived in the garden pond for a year until she relented and changed him back." Siobhán leaned close to whisper in my ear. "And honestly, you are way too cute to be turned into a frog."

I might have blushed and smiled a little as she walked away. Sabine just rolled her eyes and shook her head. "Men. You're all governed by your reproductive glands. All it takes is a cute girl in a short skirt or a pair of yoga pants, and you lose every last bit of dignity and sense you possess."

I looked at her and smiled. "Oh, you know you're the only girl for me, Sabine."

She snickered. "Right. And you're not still in love with your dead girlfriend, either." The timbre in her voice said she might not be happy with that fact, but we were just friends. I figured she was just concerned that I hadn't moved on after Jesse.

Sabine took my arm in hers and began walking me down the lecture hall steps. "C'mon, we still have time to grab a cup of coffee at the student union before your next class. I'll take notes and cover for you, while you head off to see what the wicked witch of the Southwest wants."

EIGHT

Journal Entry—Eight Months, Twenty-Five Days A.J.

It's all in my head. I'm going to talk to Dr. Larsen about increasing my meds.

-McC

AUSTIN, Texas—Present Day

After finally getting some caffeine in me, I thanked Sabine for agreeing to take notes in my midday class and headed over to Maeve's home. You'd think that the faery queen of Austin would live in a palatial mansion in the hills somewhere, but not Maeve. She preferred to be in the thick of things, so her impressive but not quite ostentatious Victorian was located on the cliffs above Riverside Drive, just west of I-35 in a tiny and expensive neighborhood next to Ladybird Lake and close to Zilker Park.

Her home would have been the envy of any well-to-do heiress or newly minted millionaire, if they wished to put their wealth on display while keeping up the false pretense of being absolutely in tune with the proletariat. Her home was easily worth ten million; homes like it in and near downtown Austin sold at a hefty premium. Still, because it was an older home that had been renovated and updated, it came across as being quaint and tasteful rather than evincing the gauche excesses that homes in the hills along Loop 360 were known to boast.

As I walked past the white picket fence and picture perfect front lawn, I admired the gingerbread house trim and handsome Victorian architecture of her home. Victorians were a rarity in Austin, not only because the style had never been popular there, but also because older homes in tony neighborhoods were so often torn down and replaced by modern monstrosities that detracted from the atmosphere of those formerly staid communities. I had to hand it to Maeve; she had an appreciation for all things old and beautiful, and by preserving this home she'd done a favor to her surrounding neighbors.

Interestingly, though, this neighborhood bordered on one of the less desirable areas in Austin. East Riverside drive wasn't exactly known for its lack of crime, and while Austin had a relatively low violent crime rate, we boasted one of the highest property crime rates in Texas. Yet the local meth heads and gang-bangers had learned to stay away from Maeve's place, as well as those of her neighbors. Things lurked here in the shadows and shrubbery that would best be avoided late at night... or any time, for that matter. I made it a point to pretend I didn't notice the troll watching me from within the limbs of a large crepe myrtle, and headed up the steps onto the wraparound porch to ring the doorbell.

Just as my finger touched the buzzer, the front door opened and Siobhán stepped into view. "Surprise, surprise. The druid actually took my advice. Maeve will be pleased."

I let out a long, slow sigh. "I keep telling you folk, I'm not a druid."

She sniffed and turned on heel, heading past the parlor and into the depths of the house. "Whatever. Come, she's expecting you."

I followed close on the heels of the fae girl, not wanting to risk getting turned around inside the place. Unlike a mundane home, the homes of the fae were known to unexpectedly connect to the lands of the sidhe, those places in the Underrealms where mortals were never meant to tread. Take one wrong turn in a home such as this one, and you might lose a few decades wandering aimlessly or being fed faery cakes and honey mead, only to later exit the place an old man.

Siobhán took me to the rear half of the house, where Maeve was busy baking. My nose told me she'd been preparing currant scones and cooking up a batch of blackberry jelly. The kitchen itself was massive, with commercial appliances and a huge center island that was currently occupied by mixing bowls and small glass bowls containing every ingredient necessary for whatever Maeve would be preparing next, all lined up in neat little rows. Despite the culinary activity, the counters and appliances were absolutely spotless, and beyond the delicious odors emanating from the oven and range, there remained little evidence she'd been mixing or cooking anything in here at all.

Maeve herself was dressed simply yet elegantly, and could've been a stand-in for any cable food show hostess, even the Martha herself. And just like Martha Stewart in her pre-prison days, her glamour was designed to radiate a subtle vibe that made her the ultimate MILF. Of course, it was intentional and part of how she drew mortals into her web of deceit and manipulation. To mortal men, she appeared to be at once both sexually desirable and motherly, a combination that few males could resist.

Maeve floated from behind the kitchen island and over to the range as I walked in the room. She didn't *literally* float, because that would be passé; but she moved with such an easy grace and confidence that she may as well have been walking on air. She flipped her flaxen, tastefully highlighted shoulder-length hair back and leaned in as she stirred a pot on the stove, taking a whiff and fanning the steam back to her nose with an elegant wave of her hand.

"Colin, come here and tell me if this looks done to you." I froze for a moment, unsure if she was trying to throw me off balance. *Off course she is, silly.* I decided to play along. She frowned at my hesitation and beckoned me with the wooden spoon in her hand. "Come on now, you know I don't bite guests. Let's put those famous druid senses to the test, and you tell me if I've over-cooked this blackberry jam."

I sauntered over to the stove and leaned in to smell the mixture that was barely bubbling on the range. Taking a deep inhalation of the wisps of steam coming up from the pot, I detected that yes, she'd cooked the mixture just to the point where it would set perfectly. I also noticed that she'd somehow managed to get it to the right consistency without adding pectin to the mixture. I closed my eyes and focused on the magical spectrum and "saw" the fine, airy weaves of magic that had been used to bind the whole process together, taking note of the skill, power, and effort that had been invested in such a commonplace task. It was clear that Maeve didn't really want my opinion on her jam. She simply wanted to remind me of how much magical power she commanded, and how expertly she could wield it. It was a subtle, but effective, message.

That was the thing about the fae. Sure, mortals could command magic, just as the fae could. But we mortals were limited in our ability to generate magical power, and without an external power source or reservoir, we would very quickly expend any endogenous magical energies we possessed. And it took a very long time to restore those magical reserves, which was why most magicians, witches, and wizards could be seen wearing various trinkets and medallions, and carrying wands, staves, and other objects of power. Such inanimate objects were used to collect and store magical energies, and could be drawn from so the mage would not need to draw on their own power to perform magic.

But the fae had no such need. Their native lands were fashioned purely of magic, and therefore there were few limits to their power. As long as they had a connection to the Underrealms, they had access to unlimited reserves of magical energy. In fact, there were really only three ways for a mortal to defeat a powerful fae:

1. You could destroy their physical body, or physically overpower them;
2. You could trick them into agreeing not to harm you;

3. Or you could cut off their connection to the Underrealms, thereby leveling the playing field and making it a fair fight.

Either way, if you had to fight a powerful fae you were screwed. Ages ago the Milesians discovered the secret to defeating the fae, a development that eventually led to the defeat of the Tuatha Dé Danann and their subsequent banishment to Underhill. As it turns out, every fae magic user's Achilles heel is this: while in the human realm, they must connect to the magic of the Underrealms through nature, namely the earth, rocks, trees, and wildlife. Amergin the druid revealed this vulnerability when he called upon the spirit of Ireland to turn against the Tuatha Dé Danann, an act which robbed them of much of their magical power. Once the land turned against the fae, they were forced to rely on their own magical reserves as any mortal would, and eventually they had to concede defeat to their human conquerors. This was, in part, why the fae both respected and feared druids and the druid-trained like me.

Why couldn't the fae use magical reservoirs like humans did? Because the best conductors and conduits for magical energies were anathema to the fae: iron, rowan wood, and mystical symbols. The fae were also known to be fascinated by glittering gems, and while they held no particular aversion to them, having such an object on their person could cause a distraction that might have disastrous results in battle. Thus, the fae avoided using inanimate objects as a source of power, preferring instead to rely on their connection to Underhill for their magical might. That was more than enough to make any fae magic user a challenge for even the most powerful human magician, witch, or wizard to defeat.

Wisely, I avoided bringing any of this up with Maeve. Instead, I minded my manners and responded exactly as Finn had taught me to when dealing with the fae, by using flattery while never thanking them or committing to any promise or oath.

"It smells lovely, and you've cooked it to perfection. The Queen of the Austin Sidhe must be the epitome of gastronomic expertise, and a more charming and graceful hostess could never be found in Underhill or above."

She smiled sweetly and removed her apron, hanging it neatly on a hook in the corner of the kitchen. As she did, I noted that her figure these days was more Giada than Martha Stewart, and that the simple yet classy blouse she wore over designer jeans and Valentino flats was left unbuttoned at the top to display an ample amount of cleavage. Her facial features were fine, with slightly upturned eyes, high cheek bones, and lips that succeeded at exuding sensuousness without being overkill. Her face and skin possessed an agelessness that was almost unsettling. She could have been 29, or 59; it was anyone's guess. It was all glamour, of course, and yet her magic was such that I was unable to see what she really looked like beneath her façade. My guess was that she was like most of the High Court fae—slightly alien in appearance, yet ethereally and unnaturally beautiful as well.

Regardless, my eyes remained level with hers at all times. Finn taught me that sexual predilections were a weakness that could and would be exploited by any fae, and showing weakness of any kind in the presence of an apex predator like Maeve could get you killed. Or worse.

After taking a moment to size me up, she spoke, breaking me out of my momentary reverie.

"Finnegas taught you well, and you do honor to the memory of the druid bards of old."

I bowed my head in appreciation of the compliment, acknowledging it without becoming indebted to her by verbally expressing my gratitude. For several seconds more she continued to appraise me, and finally her steel eyes flashed with amusement as well as a hint of ancient eldritch power held at bay.

"Well, you're no bumbling fool, that's for sure," she stated. "I must say, my spies did not exaggerate in the slightest when they reported that you were Finn's finest pupil in an age. Walk with me, boy."

NINE

Journal Entry—Eight Months, Twenty-Six Days A.J.

It's not all in my head. At least, I don't think it is. Last night, I was having my usual nightmare, the one where I run into the cave and see myself killing Jesse. I scream, I beg, I fight myself, but nothing I do can stop me from killing her.

I woke up in a cold sweat, and I swear she was standing at the foot of my bed. I mean, I couldn't see her, but I could smell her perfume, and I sensed that she was there. Maybe it's just wishful thinking, but I'm starting to believe that Jesse's ghost is haunting me.

Oh man... what if she's been around this whole time? Have I been keeping her from moving on? What if she's been trying to talk to me and I haven't been listening or paying attention? I don't know what to think about all this, but Dr. Larsen will know what to do.

Then again, I did just ask her to increase my meds. Maybe I'd better keep this all to myself. For now.
-McC

AUSTIN, Texas—Present Day

I did as Maeve asked and held out my arm to her. She casually took it in her own as she guided me where she wished to go, all while making it look as though it was my idea to lead *her* in that direction. Despite the danger I felt at her proximity, I had to admit that I found her old-school manners to be charming, if a little dated. But if I was enjoying Maeve's matronly charms so much at the moment, then why did I have the nagging suspicion she was about to castrate me with a rusty knife? I finally decided to just enjoy the moment, but to be on my guard just the same.

As we exited the kitchen, Maeve dismissed Siobhán, who'd been standing off to the side, statue-like, during our brief conversation.

"Go find something to do, dear. Buy some new clothes, or find some man to ply your charms with for a time. I'll send for you again when you're needed."

Siobhán curtsied and left the way we'd come in, sparing me an indecipherable look as she exited. Maeve gestured at her departing form.

"My granddaughter, many generations removed.

She's a smart girl, but ambitious. I daresay I'll have to watch that one in years to come."

She guided me through a grand archway and into a library with floor to ceiling bookshelves all around. The walls here, as in the rest of the house, were painted tastefully in an off-white color, and the midday sunlight lit the room up without being overpowering. Maeve patted my arm and released it, then walked up to a wall of books and chanted softly under her breath, too faintly for me to make out the words. With one wave of her hand, the wall disappeared before me to reveal a staircase leading down.

I opened the adjacent door to peek into the room beyond. On the other side was a formal dining room, making it physically impossible for there to be a stairwell behind the shelves. This was a path to Underhill, and yet I'd not even sensed the presence of the glamour or doorway, nor the many wards that Maeve was busy releasing so I could pass through unharmed.

She gestured at the doorway. "After you, my dear."

I hesitated. There were rules governing safe passage for mortals traveling the Underrealms at the behest of the fae. Maeve's brow crinkled slightly, then she looked off to the side and rolled her eyes.

"Fine. 'No harm shall come to you by entering Underhill though my demesne, nor shall you be detained by me or mine.' Happy?"

I nodded, just barely stopping myself before thanking her. "Don't slip up now, boy," she quipped as I entered the doorway and began leading the way down. "I'm just beginning to fancy you."

We descended the stairs for an unnaturally long time; how long, it was hard to say. Time was different in the Underrealms, and you could spend days or weeks there and come back only seconds after you left the mortal world. Or you might be gone for what seemed like a single day, and lose decades here in the real world. I decided to trust that Maeve wouldn't lead me into a dangerous time distortion, and kept marching down the stairs. The walls lit our way further down by emitting a pale blue luminescence, and Maeve kept my mind occupied by conversing with me about the finer points of how to plan seating arrangements for a proper dinner party.

After an indeterminate amount of time, we reached the bottom. The stairwell opened up into a hall reminiscent of the room that held Smaug's hoard in *The Hobbit*. The space itself was massive, lit by torches that burst into flames one by one as Maeve led our way through the hall and deeper into her treasury.

"Few mortals have seen this, and lived," she said simply as I followed her between piles of gold and gems. "Most of this is useless to my kind, but we use it to do trade with the dwarves and ogrish, and as a means of gaining leverage in human affairs."

As I walked behind her, I did the occasional pirou-
ette so as not to miss anything. There was wealth here
beyond imagining, enough to buy a thousand posh Victorian mansions and still have billions to spare. I was privy
to a fortune that had been amassed over several millennia, and for my part I wasn't going to waste the opportunity to gawk. Soon, however, Maeve stopped as we
reached a large iron-clad door.

"Ah, here we are."

She muttered and waved again, and as I shifted my
senses into the magical realm I saw powerful wards
releasing from the door and frame. Maeve donned a pair
of thick leather gloves that sat on a pedestal next to the
door, and they shrunk to fit her hands almost instantly.

She held her hands up and grinned like a child, eyes
twinkling as she spoke. "Wyvern skin. Difficult to get
these days, and even harder to work with. Keeps me
from feeling the effects of the iron in the door. I'd get you
to do this, but some of the wards are permanent, and I
need to keep you alive for what I'm about to ask of you.
Good help is so hard to replace, you know."

Maeve grabbed the massive door handle and pulled,
and despite her slight appearance the door moved with
surprisingly little effort on her part. It swung open to
reveal a smallish room, maybe twelve feet by twelve feet.
There was an ivory pedestal in the middle of the room,
upon which rested a crystal cube roughly one-foot

square. An empty velvet pillow with a large round indentation in its center sat inside the cube.

"Whoever took it from me was human, that's for certain. The gloves will only accept my hands, and no fae could open that door without burning their hand to a stump."

"They could have brought their own gloves," I observed.

"Wouldn't have mattered. The gloves are like a key that unlocks certain wards on the entry." She nodded at the door. "That's cold-forged dwarven steel, the very best. Now, take a good look at that display case."

I assumed she meant that I should look at it with my second sight, so I tuned into the magical frequencies once more. The magic spells and wards encasing the display nearly blinded me. Even the most powerful fae would have taken weeks to weave these protective spells, and no run of the mill mortal magician could bypass them alone. After adjusting my senses to filter out the magical glare emanating from the spells, I took a closer look at the case.

"Whoever stole this object from you didn't tamper with the wards. This is magic many degrees removed from my paltry skills, but as far as I can tell they've not been touched."

Maeve nodded. "Exactly. I've been trying to figure out how they did it since it happened. Damned if I know how they pulled it off. And let me tell you, boy, I've seen some tricks in my day."

I stood up to my full height and crossed my arms as I addressed the queen of the Austin fae. "Maeve, what in the world was in this case? What kind of weapon requires you to ward it so strongly? It was a weapon, was it not?"

She smiled. "Figured that one out, did you? Well, it wasn't an artifact as powerful as Fragarach, but it's just as dangerous in its own right." Her eyes darted to my Craneskin Bag as she mentioned the famous sword, making me wonder just how much she really knew about me.

"Fragarach, yeah right," I muttered to myself. "Like the Tuatha would be stupid enough to leave that laying around to be stolen."

Maeve ignored my muttering and continued her sales pitch. "No, my boy, what was taken from me was a priceless treasure, a weapon powerful enough to give the Tuatha of old pause. The thieves stole the Tathlum, the sling stone that old Lugh used to kill Balor himself."

I whistled softly. "The stone that killed the king of the Fomorians. That must be some weapon."

The Fomorians were the original boogeymen of ancient Irish mythology, sort of the Celtic counterparts to the Titans of Greek and Roman legend. Big, ugly, and hella mean. Anything that could take their king down was bad news, no doubt about it.

Maeve nodded in agreement. "It is. And I don't have to tell you the only reason to gain possession of such a weapon is to bring the high and mighty low."

I spared a glance at Maeve as I continued to look around. "Which begs the question, why *did* you have it? And how did you get it in the first place?"

Maeve snorted, which sounded peculiar coming from her. "In answer to your first question, for insurance. And as for the second, let's just say it was given into my hand for safekeeping by someone who was very close to the original owner, and leave it at that."

"Who else knew it was here, beside you?"

She shrugged slightly, a gesture that seemed out of place for a nearly immortal being. "No one, not even my own kin. Not that I could trust them anyway. It's dangerous at the top, you know."

I nodded and continued looking around the room for clues, using my mundane eyesight and then scanning with the second sight. After several minutes, I slapped my hands to my sides. I was as stumped as she appeared to be.

"Well, I'm not seeing any way they could've gotten in here. There's no sign that they broke your wards, even if they were capable of such a feat. And the only thing I know of that could bypass wards this strong is—"

"The Dullahan?" she asked. I nodded, and she smiled slyly. "But of course, no one's seen him in centuries, have they?"

The Dullahan, *the* Dullahan that is, was an unstoppable harbinger of death in Irish legend. He was also the so-called headless horseman from Washington Irving's story, which was based on true events. Legend had it that the Dullahan could bypass any lock, gate, door, or ward. He'd be the ultimate cat burglar and second story man, if he wasn't so preoccupied with damning his victims to a painful death and beheading them.

But why would a creature like the Dullahan have been involved? He was a harbinger of death, and unconcerned with normal, mortal affairs. Sure, he could have gotten into the room, but it just didn't make any sense. One thing was for certain, though: I didn't want to have anything to do with this mess if the Dullahan was involved.

"Well, Maeve, intrigued as I am by your problem, I don't see how I can be of any help to you. I've retired from hunting, from druidry, from being a champion—all of it. And, to be honest, you don't have enough gold in this entire treasury to change my mind.

"Besides, I don't see why you just don't get one of your own people to track this thief down. Surely you have fae in your employ who are better suited than I am for this sort of thing."

Maeve shook her head slowly from side to side. "That's the problem facing me: how can I trust that it wasn't one of my own who stole from me? By assigning one of mine to investigate, I could easily be handing this job to the very individual who took the Tathlum. No, I can't trust anyone from inside my court to handle this. It has to be an outsider."

I held my hands up. "Sorry, Maeve, but I just can't help you."

She hung her head slightly, then looked me in the eye. "Well, you can't fault me for trying. Come, let's get you back upstairs so you can give that pretty little glaistig friend of yours a break from your freshman composition professor's droning."

I allowed her to lead the way back to the stairs after she'd locked the room. Strangely, the trip up took only a fraction of the time it had taken to descend, and if I had to guess I'd say we ascended no more than a few flights of stairs at most. As we exited the magical doorway, I waited politely while Maeve reset her wards and concealment spells.

When she was finished, she addressed me with a barely detectable grin. "Colin, before you go there's one more thing I'd like you to see. Come."

Without waiting for me, she glided off into another part of the house. Once again in fear of getting lost and wandering for all eternity inside her home, I followed without comment.

Maeve spoke over her shoulder as I tagged along. "It's my art collection, you see. As I understand it, you're in a position to appreciate the arts as well as anyone. What, with your mother being a famous artist and all."

At that moment we entered a sizable room that had probably once been used to entertain guests. But now, the walls and floor were lined with paintings. Dozens of them, in fact. And I recognized each and every one—or at least who had painted them.

"These are my mom's paintings. How—"

She cut me off. "I've been a 'silent patron' of your mother for several years now. In fact, my patronage was instrumental in getting her noticed by the art world. Although, I daresay that interest in her work has waned in recent years. Were it not for the many purchases I've made of her paintings recently, it's quite possible that the woman would be destitute."

My voice dripped venom as I replied. "And since you own the majority of her work, you could ruin her, any time you choose."

Maeve nodded to me matter-of-factly. "Oh yes, I could easily flood the market with her paintings, and make her work practically worthless overnight. She'd be back to working as a legal secretary in no time. But at her age and with those long hours, well—I wouldn't recommend such a career move."

My shoulders sagged and I hung my head. Maeve had found a weakness and ruthlessly exploited it. And the infuriating thing about this turn of events was that she'd been scheming to get me in her pocket for years... and I'd never even known it.

This was exactly why I hated dealing with the fae. They were devious, absolutely merciless, arbitrary, manipulative, unpredictable—and they played the long game like nobody's business. They were very nearly immortal, after all. Trying to outsmart the fae was like trying to beat a chess grandmaster while you were blindfolded and drunk. You'd lose every time, before you'd even located your chess pieces.

"Fine. I'll do this one job for you, but once it's done it's done," I said as I squared my shoulders and stared daggers at her. She might have had me in her pocket, but what she didn't know was that I was all sharp corners and rough edges, and very hard to hold.

Maeve gave a Cheshire grin and totally ignored my obvious displeasure. She clapped her hands together, clasping them at chest level.

"Splendid! Then I suggest you start by investigating this gentleman." She reached to a side table and handed me a business card that had been sitting there since we'd entered the room. Obviously, she'd planned to bring me here all along.

I read the card aloud. "Elias Henderson, mystical conservationist?"

"Yes, the very same. My sources tell me he possesses knowledge about whoever pulled off the heist. He's either connected, or knows someone who is." She walked me to the door, and I exited without another word.

As my feet hit the front walk, she called to me from the doorway.

"And Colin?"

I glanced over my shoulder. "I know—'don't fail or else.' This ain't my first rodeo, Queen Maeve. Just tell your goons to stay out of my way. I prefer to work alone these days."

I kept walking without waiting for a reply, and heard the door latch behind me. As I left the property, I paused just long enough to flip off the troll who watched me from the bushes.

TEN

Journal Entry—Eight Months, Twenty-Eight Days A.J.

I'm convinced it's real—that she's real. I found a handprint in the fog on the shower glass this morning. Not a large one—a small, female handprint.

Okay, I don't know that it was female for sure, but it wasn't mine and I don't think it was my mom's either. She learned the hard way back when I was a teenager that she shouldn't interrupt me in the shower. Yeah, I know, gross—but hey, everybody does it.

Anyway, I think I need to do some research on this to find out whether this is really Jesse, or just an echo. Or, maybe it's a projection from my own subconscious... something I'm creating because I want her back so badly.

I'm going to take a trip into the city and visit the Cold Iron Circle's library, just to see what I can dig up.

-McC

. . .

AUSTIN, Texas—Present Day

Before I hopped on my scooter, I sent a text to Sabine to tell her I wasn't going to make it back to campus, and promised I'd make it up to her for taking notes for me in my remaining classes. I was way too keyed up to be around a lot of people right now—and besides, I needed to vent in order to clear my head.

I took a few more seconds to text Belladonna to find out where her murders had occurred, because I had a feeling that before this job was finished I was going to need her backing me up. I figured I'd better earn all the points I could get before that time came. Hopping on my scooter, I headed toward the south side of town, to a little strip center off Lamar with graffiti on the walls, potholes dotting the parking lot, and bums sleeping on the sidewalk.

One of the things I'd learned during my recovery was that avoiding violence simply did not cut the mustard for keeping me sane. I'd been born a warrior and had fighting in my blood. Besides keeping me from becoming a Celtic version of the Hulk, what the complete avoidance of violence did was make me a nervous wreck. I became edgy to the point where I went off on people for no reason, and was constantly jumping out of my skin. When I'd told Dr. Larsen about it, she suggested that I find an outlet for my aggression, and fast.

I tried long distance running, which burned off a lot of energy but still left me with an edge after the endorphin high faded. After that I tried chopping wood, doing Crossfit, training for Spartan races and a number of other high-risk, high-calorie activities that didn't involve fighting. None of them satisfied the natural urge for violence within me that was screaming for an outlet.

Thankfully, Belladonna had come to my rescue by inviting me to the dojo she trained at when she wanted to get away from work. Camelot MMA was run by a former Circle hunter by the name of Talyn. Somehow he got screwed by management a few years before he hit retirement age, so he decided to take his retirement early and go fishing instead. But like me, he couldn't get away from his natural desire to mix it up now and again.

To answer that need, he opened a dojo and started training competitive fighters by day and hunters at night. Of course, the mundane members who weren't clued in had no idea about the "special" training that Talyn offered after hours. Even so, the day classes were still hard core enough to provide me a way to blow off steam. There were enough pros and serious amateur fighters training at Camelot to give me a run for my money, and there was always an ample supply of juice heads who were there looking for some good hard sparring.

Because of the supernatural gifts I possessed I was never ever in any real danger of injury, even when facing the pro fighters. Champions, the kind who were born to fight supernatural creatures, were supernaturally tough and resilient. We were strong, fast, and agile beyond the capabilities of even elite Olympic athletes. In fact, many of the most successful pro fighters and athletes were actually champions who were either unaware of or exploiting their talents.

Still, that meant we had to tone things down when training with average mortals, and the only time I really got to rev it up was when I got matched with another hunter—which wasn't often, since most of them came to train after hours. That didn't mean I couldn't get a good workout in though, and I needed to work off some energy today. No sooner than I'd hit the front doors, I was headed back to my locker to gear up so I could throw down.

When I emerged from the locker room a few guys were already hanging out around the cage gearing up. I walked up and greeted a couple of the regulars, sizing up a beefy-looking dude that might have been Samoan or Polynesian. At about six-foot-six and three hundred and ten pounds, he was easily the largest person at the gym today. I was no tiny dancer, coming in at six-foot-one and two hundred, but this guy was a monster. He'd do.

After some casual introductions I found out his

name was Hemi. He'd been fighting competitively in his native New Zealand, but he'd recently moved to Texas looking for bigger fights and better training opportunities. He asked me what I liked better, kickboxing or ground work, and I told him we could just mix it up doing full MMA sparring and see where that took us. He smiled and said that was fine by him.

We entered the ring and touched gloves, and started off with a light round of technical sparring to warm-up. Hemi was quick for a big man, and had good Muay Thai striking skills as well as some pretty smooth takedowns. But, like many big men, I could see that his jiu-jitsu was weak. He mostly relied on ground and pound techniques that involved smashing his opponents into the canvas. I tucked that info away as the bell struck at the end of our warm-up round, and waited for the next round to begin.

It was unspoken but understood that we'd increase the contact in the next round, and the big Maori wasn't shy about trading leather. He stepped in immediately with a whip-fast jab cross combo followed by a high right round kick that very nearly connected with my head. I parried his punches and danced back as his foot whizzed by me, and proceeded to take the fight back to him with a series of punches and low kicks designed to get me some respect. Before long, we were trading blows and working each other pretty good, then the bell rang and we went back to our "corners."

Hemi was in damned good shape, as evidenced by the fact that he wasn't even breathing hard as he came out for the third round. He probed my defense using his jab and long reach, then he surprised me by coming in under my punch combo with a single leg takedown that was nearly textbook. Soon I was scrambling on my back and Hemi was raining blows down on me like Goibniu hammering away at his forge. I weathered the storm and pulled him into a closed guard position, not wanting to play open guard with such a giant of a man. As soon as I did, Hemi stood up and slammed me on the canvas, once, twice, and a third time for good measure.

Well, this is turning out to be a pretty decent match, I thought as my head bounced off the canvas a final time. By this point he was in need of a breather, since all that effort had taken a lot out of him. So, moved my hips out slightly and transitioned to his back while he was winded. I pounded on him a little bit from back mount, because he was smart and guarded his neck fairly well, but eventually he gave me an opening and I was able to choke him into submission.

After he tapped, we went a few more rounds. In the final round he caught me with a left hook, right cross, switch round kick combo that knocked me silly. I had to hand it to him: for a big guy he could really move. I recovered, and we stalemated in the clinch until the buzzer sounded.

Five rounds was enough for me, and I decided to call it quits and head home. Hemi stopped me when I exited the locker room and shook my hand.

"You got a mean right hand, and your jiu-jitsu is sick as, yeah? Why don't I see your name on any of the fight rosters for coming events?"

I smiled. "Well, I'm retired."

"You look awful young to be retired, cuz." Hemi wasn't dumb, apparently.

"I decided to go to school instead of pursuing a career in fighting. Keep my mom off my back."

He nodded. "Yeah, nah bro, I get it. Next time you wanna smash though, you let me know, yeah?"

"Same here, Hemi. And if you need anyone to show you around town, just ask Talyn for my number. He knows how to find me."

"Chur—I mean thanks, mate." We did the bro hand-shake, and as I did my fingers brushed one of the elaborate tattoos on his forearm. I felt a slight shock as a powerful ward or spell woven into the tattoo reacted to my touch. It'd been covered up by Hemi's rash guard while we'd been rolling, which was probably why I hadn't noticed it before.

I knew little about Maori culture or folklore, so I didn't know what to make of the big man's magic. I decided to just let it go, because he was obviously a nice guy and he might not even know he was magically warded. For all I knew, he had a family member or friend who was a shaman and just trying to keep him safe. I wished him well and headed back to the junkyard to regroup and determine my next steps.

ELEVEN

Journal Entry—Nine Months, One Day A.J.

Well, that went well. Apparently I am persona non grata with those Cold Iron Circle jerks.

Hah! "Circle jerks." See what I did there?

Anyway, when I showed up at their HQ, you'd have thought that the devil himself had walked through their doors. No sooner had I hit the lobby in their building then they had a group of black clad security types escorting me out. Forcefully. It was quite a scene. Since they occupy the top four floors of an office building in downtown Austin, all secret and unbeknownst to the mundane inhabitants, I had a captive audience of a few dozen office workers as they walked me outside like some crazy person.

Long story short, it seems they consider me to be some

sort of magical nuclear weapon, and one with a hair-trigger detonator. Hashtag fml, right?

Anyway, I met this really cool Circle hunter in training at La Crème, a coffee shop just a few blocks down from their headquarters. I walked in there to regroup and mope, and while I was lost in my cappuccino she plopped down at my table and started chatting me up. Said she saw what had happened, and that it was total bullshit how they'd treated me.

I think she was coming on to me, but I'm not positive. Jesse was my first and only, well, you know. So I don't have much experience with women. One thing's for sure though: I am not ready to get into another relationship. Especially not while I'm still working things out with Jesse's memory.

And, potentially, her ghost.

Where was I? Oh yeah. So this hunter, Belladonna, has offered to help me do my research. When I told her what was going on, she was cool enough to not give me the look. You know, that look everyone gives you when they find out you recently suffered a major tragedy? Yeah, that look.

Well, just the fact that she's not treating me with kid gloves has won me over to her. I'm going to take her up on her offer, and see if we can figure out what's going on with my ghost... or whatever.

Maybe it's all in my head. I haven't decided yet.

-McC

P.S. Dr. Larsen says I "deflect" and "compartmentalize my emotions" with humor and sarcasm. Maybe so, but if it keeps me from going all Mr. Hyde again, call me Dane freaking Cook.

AUSTIN, Texas—Present Day

The next morning, I woke up a bit sore from the rounds I'd done with Hemi, but felt a lot less angry and in a better frame of mind for finding Maeve's thief. After making some instant coffee (nasty, but caffeinated), I opened my laptop and pulled out the card Maeve had given me. Elias Henderson worked for a group that called themselves CIRCE, which apparently stood for *Cryptid International Rescue CollectivE*. While their website was vague as to how they went about rescuing creatures that officially didn't exist, their contact page listed an address that was off West 15th—well within scooter distance.

Since I didn't have any classes on Tuesdays and Thursdays, I decided there was no time like the present to see what the hell these folks were up to. I grabbed my Craneskin Bag—checking to make sure I had a few goodies and surprises handy inside that great big spatial anomaly within—and went to see what CIRCE was about.

As soon as I arrived at the address on the website, it became clear that someone with a lot of money was bankrolling this operation. Their offices comprised both floors of a rezoned and converted two-story home that was easily worth a cool million. And while they weren't exactly advertising their location with a huge sign, their logo was etched in the front door glass for all to see. Intrigued, I parked my scooter and walked up the front walk like I belonged there. Since I didn't see anyone spying on me from inside, I quickly walked behind the building to poke around before I made my presence officially known.

Around the back of the building, I found a small parking area containing three late-model vehicles painted white with the CIRCE logo on the sides. One was an SUV, another was a panel van, and a third was a 24-foot moving truck. There was nothing to indicate what they used the vehicles for, or why they might have needed to have a company moving truck, for that matter. Finding nothing else of interest, I went back to the front of the building and walked in like I was supposed to be there.

Before I got three steps into the foyer, a shrill voice called out from a doorway off to my right. "Oh, you must be the intern from the university! Come on in here, and I'll be right with you."

I walked into the office and saw a plump, middle-aged woman with long, dirty-blonde braids sitting behind a desk with a phone receiver held up to her ear. The placard on her desk read "Margie Reynolds, Operations Coordinator." She was wearing a tie-dye shirt with the CIRCE logo on the front, and behind her was a map of the U.S. with a variety of colored stick pins adorning it. She covered the mouthpiece and mouthed "Sorry," then pointed to a water cooler and dorm fridge behind me and gestured I should take a seat. I did.

I heard someone talking rather excitedly on the other end of the line. The woman nodded as she replied. "Yes, Mr. Graves, we've dealt with this sort of thing before. Mm-hmm, we have quite a bit of experience with amphibious creatures. Yes, they will keep eating your cattle, so I suggest that you remove those animals from the area and pasture them somewhere else until we can get a team out there. No, I don't have an estimate of when that will be just yet, but I'll have one by this afternoon. Thank you for your patience. We'll be in touch."

She hung up the phone and let out a long breath. "Phew! That man was really upset about his cattle." Margie stood up and reached across the desk to shake my hand. "Margie Reynolds, and you must be—"

"Colin, Colin McKenzie. Pleased to meet you, Margie."

Margie blinked a few times. "Oh, they told me they were sending a Kyle something or other, but that he wouldn't be here until the second or third week of classes."

I decided to gamble on a wild-ass guess. "Kyle took an intern position with the San Antonio zoo, so they gave me his place. But I can start today, if that's okay."

Margie smiled. "Wonderful! Most of our staff is out in the field at the moment, but our director, Elias, is around here somewhere. I'll get your paperwork started, and when Elias comes in he can handle your orientation. Sound good?"

I nodded, and spent the next half-hour filling out employee intake forms with false information. Roughly the same time I finished, Elias walked in from the back and stood in the office doorway. Elias was medium height and build, nothing spectacular, with a man bun and wire-frame glasses. He wore a tan safari shirt with the CIRCE logo and an embroidered name tag, green cargo shorts, and Teva sandals.

Margie introduced me. "Elias, this is your new intern, Colin. Colin, this is Elias. He's our director, and heads up our field teams."

I stood and shook hands with him. "Ah, good," he remarked, "they finally sent us an intern with some muscle. Some of the equipment we use is pretty heavy—shouldn't give you too much trouble, though."

He looked at Margie. "When he's done here, can you send Colin to the staging area?"

"He's already finished," Margie stated. "Why don't you take him out back and start his orientation now?"

Elias nodded. "Alright. Follow me, Colin."

I trailed him down a short hall to a room that housed a number of large wire animal traps, as well as several man-sized cages welded out of angle iron and heavy steel mesh. The walls were lined with cattle prods, stun guns, tranquilizer guns, pneumatic net cannons, and animal control poles like the kind dog catchers used. Elias held his arms out and spun around in a circle.

"This is our ready room, where we stage our teams before they head out to the field. Now, I hear you already have some field experience working with larger animals. Is that correct?"

"You might say that," I said and nodded. "Sure."

He walked behind a desk and sat down, then smiled again reassuringly. "Well, if you didn't already you'll get plenty here, don't worry about that. We handle about three, maybe four cases a month. Sometimes they're real cryptids, while other times it's just a wild hog, a gator, or the odd mountain lion."

I raised my hand. "Excuse me—you said cryptids, right? As in mythological creatures?"

"Oh they didn't tell you? We're on the cutting edge of research here at CIRCE, real mind-blowing stuff. The animals and species we deal with are unlike anything you'll ever see in the academic world, and that's because we're the premier rescue and relocation operation for cryptids in the country. We take calls from all over. If they're in Texas, New Mexico, Louisiana, or Oklahoma we usually drive to the incident site. But we have a chopper and a converted military transport plane on standby as well."

"But you said 'cryptids.' I'm still not sure exactly what you mean by that."

Elias' eyes got wide, and he gesticulated freely as he spoke. "Oh, it's really quite exciting! Now, don't think you're going to see one of these creatures on your first field expedition, but with the call volume we're experiencing you'll definitely see one your first month."

He began marking off species on his fingers as he spoke. "We've handled sasquatches, lycanthropes, vampires, a unicorn—you don't see those every day—two chupacabras, a cockatrice, a wampus cat... and just last month we relocated a pair of selkies who were harassing crab fishing outfits off the coast of Alaska. *Dangerous Catch* indeed!" He struck the desk lightly with his fist, flashing me a cheesy grin.

I nearly did a spit take with my water when I heard the word *relocated*. "Wait a minute—what do you mean 'relocate'?" I asked.

He leaned back in his chair and placed his hands behind his head. "Oh, we relocate all the cryptids we capture. Yes, our operation is purely catch and release.

Our mission is to *preserve* the cryptid population for the benefit of future generations."

I leaned forward and placed both hands on his desk. "Let me get this straight—you're *capturing* vampires and werewolves, and relocating them? Where could you possibly take them that you can be certain they won't kill again?"

He frowned slightly at the tone of my voice. "You seem to know a lot about this sort of thing for a college student. Did Professor Cooper take my advice and start integrating a cryptid module into his course material?"

I shrugged. "I'm a dual major—anthropology and biology."

Elias bobbed his head side to side. "Interesting choice for a dual-major. You should talk to Margie about career opportunities with CIRCE after your internship.

"Now, to answer your question—of *course* we're capturing them. I mean, what are we supposed to do, shoot them dead? These are endangered species we're talking about here. And I think it goes without saying, whenever human expansion encroaches on the natural habitat of a predator species, there are going to be some casualties, no doubt about it. But it's not the animal's fault—they're just doing what comes natural to them."

I sighed and shook my head. "You do realize that these creatures are capable of higher thought processes, right? I mean, they're able to rationalize, and in most cases are just as intelligent if not more so than human beings."

He slapped his hands on the desk. "I know, isn't it great? They're absolutely fascinating. I mean, I could just sit and stare at a werewolf all day. They're so feral, and yet so free." He leaned in and whispered conspiratorially behind his hand. "Just between you and me, I've thought more than once about climbing into a cage with one and letting them turn me. But don't tell Marge."

I resisted the urge to roll my eyes, and spoke with a dead serious look on my face. "I'm sure that wouldn't turn out poorly for you at all."

Elias threw his hands up and clapped them together with glee. "Right? Who wouldn't want super-strength and a few hundred years added to their lifespan?"

"Um, someone who wasn't clinically insane?" I whispered under my breath, perhaps a little too loudly.

He did a double-take and laughed. "Oh, you're funny Colin. You're going to get on great here, for sure."

I sat down and placed my head in my hands. "Elias, can I ask what happened to the last intern who worked for you?"

Elias looked perplexed. "How did you know—? Oh, of course. You had to have replaced someone, right? Rest assured, that young man's family is being taken care of financially. We are *very* well funded, and our sponsors have deep pockets."

"That's—comforting to know," I replied. "Say, is there a restroom around here?"

"Sure, right up the hall and to the left. You can't miss it."

"Great. Be right back." At this point I still had no idea whether Elias was directly involved with the theft of the Tathlum. However, my gut told me that it was unlikely, because he seemed way too clueless to pull off a heist like that. What I was sure of, though, was that he was batshit crazy.

That being said, there was no way an operation like this was running off donations from grateful clients. From the sound of it, whoever was bankrolling them was both loaded and connected. CIRCE didn't advertise publicly—who would believe them if they did?—and yet they were still being contacted regularly to handle supernatural creature infestations and sightings. So, what I wanted to know was, who was pulling the strings behind the scenes?

I headed down the hall toward the bathroom, and since there wasn't a soul in sight I decided to sneak upstairs. I'd lucked out by showing up on a day when no one was around but Elias and Margie, so the second floor was completely unoccupied. I wandered around for a minute or so until I found a room labeled "Records and Accounting." *Locked.* I cast a minor cantrip to unlock the door and ducked inside.

Within a few minutes I'd located financial statements that indicated their bills were being paid by an entity calling itself "The Ananda Corporation." I snapped some pictures of the documents with my cell phone, then straightened everything up and headed back downstairs. When I reentered the staging area, Elias was engrossed in looking at hentai on his laptop. He either didn't realize I could see the reflection in his glasses, or he just didn't care. *Nasty.*

He glanced up from the computer screen to acknowledge my presence. "Oh, hey man, I thought for sure you'd bailed on us."

I feigned surprise. "Me? No way, this is the internship of my dreams. Naw, I just think I ate some bad tacos this morning. You mind if we pick this up tomorrow?"

Elias shrugged. "Sure, no problem. Not much going in here. Margie just got a call from a rancher out in LaGrange who has some kappa eating his cows, but I'll wait to check it out so you can ride along. Meet me here tomorrow around this time, and we'll head out to the field so you can catch your first cryptid!"

I bent my arm and made a fist, then punched the air in front of my chest. "Elias, I can hardly wait."

TWELVE

Journal Entry—Nine Months, Three Days A.J.

Yeah, it's definitely Jesse's ghost. Belladonna called yesterday and let me know that she found a few texts with entries that might shed some light on my situation. So, since Mom was working and I was without wheels for the day (the joys of being jobless and living at home, right?) she offered to drive out and bring the books with her so we could look them over together.

Things were cool at first. We were checking out the texts, totally not with anything else in mind—at all—and then Belladonna laid her hand on my arm to stop me from turning a page.

That's when all the glasses in the kitchen shattered at once.

Belladonna looked at me, I looked at her, and she politely and calmly suggested that she should probably go.

She left the books with me, and wisely left without so much as a "see you later."

After Belladonna had gone, I said to no one in particular that Belladonna didn't mean anything by it, and she was only trying to help.

So, now I have to buy my mom a whole new set of dinnerware.

Yep, my girlfriend is haunting me.
-McC

AUSTIN, Texas—Present Day

I spent the rest of the day doing online research on this mysterious Ananda Corporation. From what I could tell, they billed themselves as a venture capital firm that mainly invested in biotech and medical research. Why they'd be paying the bills for CIRCE was beyond me; Investopedia said VC firms normally just fronted start-ups the money they needed to get through the incubator stage, and then they'd stay behind the scenes until it was time to sell their stock at a fat profit—that is, if the company they'd invested in had a decent public stock offering.

It just didn't make sense for a VC firm to be involved with what was basically a non-profit animal rescue operation. Sure, the "animals" they were rescuing were actually supernatural creatures, and for the most part those creatures were sociopathic killers, but by all appearances CIRCE wasn't in it for the money. Along with all the crazy that was necessary to motivate a group of people to capture and relocate some of the most dangerous species on the planet, there was a whole lot of weird going on that I just didn't understand.

Which meant I was going to go kappa hunting with Elias tomorrow morning. Hoo. Ray.

I decided that the best therapy for the anger I currently felt over being blackmailed into working for Maeve was caffeine, and lots of it. Besides, I thought I might need to do some recon with Belladonna that night, to help her with her little werewolf problem. I figured I may as well get a head start on staying up late, so I munched on some ramen and tuna, brushed my teeth to get rid of the tuna breath, and headed over to La Crème.

Once there, I ordered a red eye (twelve ounces of black coffee and two shots of espresso, thank you very much) and texted Sabine. I owed her for covering for me, and figured the least I could do was buy her a drink to say thanks. Along with slinging java, Luther served beer and wine—which made sense since most paranormals liked to drink. It took a lot of alcohol to get some species drunk, so he made a killing serving craft brews and wines from the Texas Hill Country to yuppies, hipsters, and supernaturals alike.

Luther let me purchase alcohol even though I was

not yet of age, and I had a pint of Thirsty Goat waiting for Sabine when she arrived. She fluttered up to the table wearing a peasant blouse, a rather loud and colorful sarong, and various non-metallic beads and bangles. Her hair was pulled back in a style that reminded me of some eighties pop star, but I couldn't remember the singer's name. I ignored the scars on her arms as she plopped down in front of me without saying a word, choosing instead to down half the pint I'd bought her before speaking.

She smiled and wiped her upper lip on her shirt sleeve like a pirate. I chuckled. Some guys liked girls who were all ribbons and curls, but give me a girl who could chug a pint. I'd take a brassy girl who could drink any day of the week over some wine sniffing tea sipper. And being half-fae, Sabine could drink most mortal guys under the table.

"That almost makes up for you bailing on me yesterday. Almost. Now, loop me in, odd one. What's up with Maeve, and why did she want to see you so badly yesterday?"

Sabine was one of the few people who knew what had really happened between Jesse and me. The Odd Thomas references were her way of putting me at ease about it. I mean, who wouldn't want to be compared to Odd Thomas? And besides, I cried like a baby when Stormy died—and that was long before I'd lost Jesse.

I gave Sabine a sobering look and took a deep breath, letting it out quickly while rubbing the stubble on my chin. "The bitch blackmailed me into working for her. Can you believe it?"

Sabine frowned and took another slug of her beer. "Of course I can believe it. She's fae, for Lugh's sake, and a faery queen besides. Maeve probably had designs on you while you were still in the womb." She slammed her pint glass down on the table, spilling the frothy contents all over her hand—despite the fact that it was three-quarters empty.

"Ugh! You should never have gone over there. I knew when I saw Siobhán sitting in that lecture hall that trouble was brewing." She wiped her hand and sat back, pulling her feet up under her in her chair. "So, what's the job?"

"I'm retrieving a magic rock that someone stole from her. Based on what she told me, it's an artifact of some significance. She suspects the theft could have been an inside job."

Sabine sipped her beer, nursing it while she thought. "Hmmm. The intrigues of the faery courts are legendary. I'd say there's a good possibility of that being the case, if losing that stone might make Maeve look bad to someone important. A faery king or queen's power is as much based on the respect of their subjects as it is on the raw power they wield. You should find out who gave

Maeve that stone in the first place. It might help point you to who stole it from her."

She had a good point. "Maeve seemed fairly reticent about sharing the details of how the stone came into her possession, but I bet Siobhán might know something."

Sabine snorted. "Siobhán is probably involved. She's nothing if not ambitious."

"Yeah, I'd think Maeve might already suspect her, if she didn't favor her so much. Siobhán seems to be her favorite grandchild, at the moment."

"Well, be careful around her. Maeve probably favors her to keep her close, so she can keep an eye on her."

I gave Sabine a mock two-finger salute. "Duly noted. You ready for another one?"

"Five minutes ago. Sure you have the funds, though?"

"Yeah, Ed gave me an advance on my pay. Most of it is going to books and gas, but I can spare a few bucks for keeping my best friend happy and slightly drunk."

"Alright, one more round—then the drinks are on me."

Sabine, like most of the higher fae, came from a family who was loaded. Money wasn't important to her, but she was considerate enough to empathize with my financial situation. Even so, she allowed me the dignity of buying her the odd cup of coffee, or splitting the check when we went out. But that didn't mean I wouldn't let her buy me a drink if I was dead broke. We enjoyed a few more rounds of coffee and beer while we went over the notes she'd taken for me.

Soon after we'd finished our third round, we heard the throaty rumble of a Harley coming from the alley behind the coffee shop. Sabine gave me a look that could've curdled milk.

"If that's who I think it is, I'll see you tomorrow morning at class." She hastily gathered her things and stood up.

"Um, I won't be making it. I have to follow up on a lead for this Maeve thing I'm working on. The sooner I get this case solved, the better."

She winked at me and smiled slyly. "Don't sweat it, I got you covered. Turns out that bitch who was shushing you the other day sells notes online. I hacked her email account and got you copies of the study outlines she's using. Apparently not much has changed since her older sister graduated four years ago."

"Sabine, you shouldn't have. I don't know what to say."

"Meh, say nothing. I figured you were going to be tied up for a while with whatever Maeve was brewing, so I took some initiative. Besides, there's no damned way I was going to cover all your classes for the next few days. I mean, I like you, Colin, but not that much."

I chuckled as I stood up and gave her a quick hug. "You're the best."

"And don't you forget it." She crinkled her nose and her eyes narrowed. "I smell trouble coming. See you when I see you." She bustled out of the place, turning up the juice on her see-me-not spell just as Belladonna was coming in the back door.

"Loverboy!" she shouted for everyone to hear as she walked through the door. "Just the man I wanted to see."

"Hey, Bells, what's up?" She puckered her full red lips and made an "oh" face as she swaggered over to me.

"So, we're doing nicknames again, are we? Grrrr, I think I'll call you 'Tiger' from here on out." She reached up and pinched my cheek like I was a school-aged boy. Which, to be honest, was exactly how I felt at the moment.

"Please don't do that," I pleaded as I plopped back into the fluffy chair I'd been occupying and took a swig of cold coffee. The twinkle in her eye told me she'd been trying to get a rise out of me, and succeeded. I decided to change the subject.

"So how goes the wolf hunt?"

She sat in the seat Sabine had been sitting in just moments before, and turned her nose up as she sniffed the space around her.

"Ugh, I smell Frumpy McFrumperson's nasty patchouli and jasmine body spray, all over these seat cushions." Belladonna sat up quickly and moved to the chair next to me. "Ah, much better. Surely you know that fae girl isn't right for you?"

My face felt hot as I hid behind my coffee cup and mumbled.

"What was that, loverboy? I couldn't hear you with your face buried in that mug. And what are you drinking, coffee? I swear, I'm going to convert you to Kentucky bourbon yet, if it's the last thing I do."

She looked around to find Luther behind the counter, and held two fingers up as she pointed at the table in front of her. The old vampire rolled his eyes and tossed a towel over his shoulder, flipping her off as she turned away. Vamps didn't care for Circle members that much, and Belladonna was fairly oblivious to the fact she was ordering one of the most powerful vampires in the city around like a chump. He more or less put up with Bells, but that was bound to piss him off. For someone who was so good at her job, she was damned clueless at times.

Luther sashayed over and set another coffee down in front of me, and plopped a Michelob light down in front of Bells. "Looks like you've put on a few pounds, so I thought I'd help you watch your figure," he stated cattily.

He turned to me and crossed his arms. "That's decaf, by the way. If you get any more caffeine in you, you won't sleep for a week."

"My my, aren't we in a tizzy today," Belladonna replied, touching up her make-up with her compact. "What's the matter, Luther, going through a dry spell? I'm happy to give you some tips—we can fix that wardrobe right up. I'll have you swimming in suitors in no time."

Luther clucked his tongue lightly against the roof of his mouth and let out a sigh. "It's called a classic look, sugar, and I'm just blending in. You should try it sometime. Good night, girl, you're dressed sluttier than half the local nest whores I've seen."

He turned on heel and walked off before Belladonna could reply. She chose to ignore his last comment, instead closing her compact with a *clack* and returning it to the snazzy leather handbag she'd placed on the seat next to her. I caught a flash of chrome inside the purse as she placed the compact within—one of probably a half-dozen firearms she had secreted on her person at any given time. I'd stopped asking where she'd hidden them all; the answers she provided created too many additional questions that I didn't care to have answered.

She leaned in and crinkled her nose. "He sure is cranky today. Is he getting laid? I mean, really—nest whores? I wear real leather, not that naugahyde and pleather crap." She took a sip of beer and waved the bottle at me as she sat back in her chair and crossed her legs, bouncing one high-heeled, steel-toed motorcycle boot up and down rhythmically.

"And you were saying? About that cow who is obviously no good for you?"

"I was hoping you'd let that go. Now, about that werewolf problem you're having—"

She cut me off mid-sentence. "Speaking of getting laid, when was the last time you got some? You look pretty uptight yourself. I bet that fae girl doesn't put out, does she?"

She swigged her beer and grinned, because I was blushing like no one's business. I stuck my fingers in my ears and closed my eyes.

"La-la-la-la-la, I'm not listening to you, la-la-la-la-la!"

She must've leaned across the table while my eyes were closed, because I felt her slap me on the arm. "Alright, you big baby, take your fingers out of your ears so we can talk. You're such a prude, sheesh."

I opened my eyes and pulled my fingers out of my ears. "Thank you. Now, would you please tell me what you found out?"

"Sure thing. Seems that our mystery wolf is stalking people in and around Zilker and Town Lake."

I rubbed my jaw and ran my hand around the back of my neck. That was definitely not good news. "That's right in Maeve's backyard."

She made a gun with her finger and thumb, pointing

it at me and dropping the hammer. "Bingo. And guess what else I found out?"

"Don't tell me—the dead bodies are all fae?"

She took a long pull off her beer and set it down. "Yep. So tell me, why in the hell would the local were-wolf Pack be killing members of Maeve's court, and right under her nose?"

I chewed my thumbnail to help me think. It was a benefit of being of the MacCumhaill line; I inherited a bit of Fionn's otherworldly wisdom, which was a perk he'd stolen from Finnegas by accident when they first met. Fionn had to suck on his thumb to activate it, because he'd burned his thumb on the Salmon of Wisdom and... well, long story short I chewed my thumbnail to avoid the uncomfortable stares that one got when sucking one's thumb in public.

I pulled my thumb away from my mouth and tapped my chin. "I'm thinking someone in Maeve's court is planning a coup, and they're taking out her most stalwart supporters. Maybe they hired the Pack to do it for them, or they're just making it look that way to start a war and further weaken her position."

Belladonna shook her head. "I'm not convinced. I lean toward simple explanations, and Occam's Razor says it's the Pack. Care to tag along with me while I go have a chat with Samson?"

Samson was the local alpha. I didn't know him

except by reputation, but he was said to be a ruthless but fair leader. "I know you can take care of yourself, but there's no way I'd ever let you walk into that clubhouse alone. Of course I'll tag along."

"Alright then, loverboy. But you'll have to ride bitch, cause I'm not letting you embarrass me, riding next to my hog on that silly scooter of yours."

THIRTEEN

Journal Entry—Nine Months, Four Days A.J.

I stayed up all night talking to Jesse. I mean, she couldn't really answer back or anything, but I'm pretty sure I felt her presence. I just kept apologizing and saying how sorry I was.

Then, I heard a squeaking noise coming from outside. I looked out the window, and there was nothing there. But as I leaned in to get a better look, my breath fogged up the glass—that's when I saw her message.

Written in the glass, there were just four words.

"love always no regrets"

I cried myself to sleep, and I can't stop crying today. But it feels... good. Cathartic. I know she's here with me, and that's all that matters.

-McC

. . .

AUSTIN, Texas—Present Day

Bells and I stood in the alley behind the coffee shop and argued for a good five minutes.

"There's nothing wrong with my scooter!" I bellowed.

"It's a freaking scooter, dork. The whole *thing* is wrong. Why can't you ride a Harley or a rice rocket like a normal hunter, or drive a classic muscle car? I mean, you'd look damned good in a '69 Chevelle Super Sport. Real nice, in fact." She looked me up and down hungrily, tapping her lower lip with one long fingernail.

I threw my hands up in the air. "And how in the world am I supposed to afford that?"

She sighed. "Duh, by hunting. Look, I know this is a sore subject with you, but from what I can tell you have your, your—" she waved a finger around in the air in my general direction "—curse thingy under control. Not only that, but you *live* in a junkyard. Can't that fat uncle of yours let you cobble together a respectable muscle car out of all that junk?"

"Whatever, I'm tired of arguing with you. Fine, I'll ride bitch back. But don't blame me when we ride up and the Pack laughs at your backup."

"No more than they would if you rode up on that little scooter." She tossed me a helmet. "Now hop on, loverboy, and hang onto me tight. Wouldn't do to have you fall off and scar up that pretty face."

She winked and dropped the visor on her helmet, and revved up the bike so I couldn't offer a snarky response. I sighed and climbed on the back, hugging her tightly because I'd seen how she rode. Her bike was a modified Night Rod Special, and she squeezed every bit of performance she could out of the thing.

Twenty-five minutes later, we pulled up to a dive bar off 183, out on the edge of an industrial area that was mostly warehouses, chain-link fences topped by barbed wire, and concrete. As soon as the bike stopped I jumped off and yanked off my helmet.

"Oh, sweet mother of mercy, don't ask me to ride with you again. You nearly got us killed—twice!"

She grabbed the helmet from me and tossed her hair back, checking herself in one of the bike's rear views. "You're still in one piece, so suck it up, cupcake. Besides, they have eyes on us already, so chill."

I looked up and sure enough, two huge dudes wearing dirty jeans, boots, biker leathers, and the club's colors were standing on either side of the front door, both of them eyeing us up and down. I knew they could hear our conversation, even though we were a good thirty feet away. One leaned into to the other and called me a pussy, and they both snickered.

Great first impression, Colin. Way to go, I thought.

Belladonna heard them too and chuckled to herself. "Just follow my lead and try to look mean. By the way, can you leave that man purse behind? It kind of ruins the whole 'I'm a big muscular Irish dude who can take care of business' thing you have going on."

I plucked at my Craneskin Bag. "This? Trust me, you'll be glad I brought it along if things go sideways in there."

She shook her head. "Whatever. I gave up trying to make you look butch a long time ago. C'mon, pretty boy, let's go see what Samson knows about these corpses that keep popping up. Follow my lead and don't get into a staring contest with anyone."

"I know how to handle myself around wolves, Belladonna," I protested quietly as we approached the door.

She marched right up and got chest to chest, or more like chest to stomach, with the one on the right. This guy had a good five inches on me, and could've given Hemi a run for his money in the huge mother-trucker department. He sported a bushy red beard with gray streaks in it, and was grizzled and scarred up like he'd seen some miles. He carried himself with supreme confidence, and had a feral look to him—even though he and his buddy were both still in human form.

I noticed he was wearing a "one-percenter" patch over a "sergeant at arms" patch on the left side of his vest. The other guy was wearing an "enforcer" patch. *Interesting.* Usually an MC like this would have two prospects guarding the door, not the head enforcer and one of his hit men. Apparently they were expecting trouble.

Belladonna wasted no time making her intentions known. "We're here to see Samson, on official Circle business."

The sergeant at arms sniffed and looked bored. "Don't give a rat's ass what you want or who you're with. The pres' ain't seein' no one tonight. We got club business to take care of, so you two ladies can kindly fuck off and come back tomorrow."

I heard a lot of yelling and cat-calling coming from inside the club, and it sounded more like they were throwing someone a bachelor party than having a serious meeting. But with outlaw bikers you never could tell. They tended to mix business with pleasure as a rule, so this guy was probably telling the truth.

I laid a hand on Belladonna's shoulder. "C'mon, let's just do what he says and come back another time."

She shook my hand off. "I'm not leaving until I talk to Samson. Tell him I'm willing to pay the entry fee."

He shook his head. "Hardbelly or no, bitches don't pay the entry fee. Club rules."

She nodded over her shoulder to me. "That's what he's here for."

The grizzled old biker looked me up and down and

shrugged. "His funeral." He stepped out of the way to let us pass. "Ask for Sonny, he'll hook you up."

We walked inside the rowdy clubhouse, and I tapped Belladonna on the shoulder as we entered. "What did I just get volunteered for?" I yelled.

She yelled back at me over the background noise, which consisted of loud Southern rock and a lot of jeering and cheering for some chick in a bikini dancing on the bar.

"Nothing major, just a little light sparring with whoever they think can whip your ass. Since they'll probably size you up to be a creampuff, it should be no problem for you."

"Right, so I'm going hand-to-hand with an outlaw biker werewolf. No big deal." I hoped she got the sarcasm in my voice, but it went right over her head.

She turned to clap me on the shoulder. "That's the spirit! You probably won't even need that many stitches when they're through with you."

Before I could respond she headed off through the crowd to the end of the bar, where she flagged down the bartender. "I need to see Sonny!" she hollered.

The lady behind the bar pointed to a guy sitting a few seats down. He was a slim, bald man with earrings in both ears, clean cut except for a pierced soul patch under his lip. Like most of the guys in this place, he was inked up like the illustrated man, sporting full sleeves on both arms as well as tats on his neck and bald head. I spotted some prison tats; he'd done hard time. Belladonna walked up behind him and tapped him on the shoulder.

Sonny turned around and glanced at both of us, and his face lit up in a grin. "Well hello, what do we have here? You looking for a date, or to score? I take American Express, blow jobs and cash, by the way."

Belladonna wasn't fazed at all by his forward and crass manner, and she leaned in to yell in his ear. "We're here to see Samson. I told your sergeant at arms we were willing to pay the entry fee."

He looked me up and down and shook his head. "You sure college boy here is up for it? He looks like a bit of a sissy to me."

I crossed my arms and tried to look tough, but my torn up jeans, Converse high tops, and "Whiskey for Breakfast" t-shirt definitely weren't helping matters. Add to that the Craneskin Bag I had slung over my shoulder, and I looked pretty out of place in a biker bar. Belladonna just smiled.

"Trust me, he can handle it."

Sonny nodded and reached behind the bar to pull out an airhorn, which he blasted overhead to get everyone's attention. Within seconds, the music turned down and all eyes fell on Sonny.

He spoke loudly, projecting his voice despite the

sudden quiet in the room. "Listen up, we got someone who wants to pay the entry fee!"

The club erupted in wild cheering and yelling; apparently, the Pack enjoyed a good fight. I leaned against the bar and waited for the cheering to die down, trying to look like I could handle myself. As soon as it did, Sonny leaned in and asked me my name and what club I was associated with.

"Colin McCool, no affiliation."

Belladonna leaned over and quickly interjected. "He's the Junkyard Druid—don't let him tell you any different."

The look on Sonny's face went from amusement to respect. He nodded once, then turned back to the crowd. "Colin McCool of the Junkyard Druids will be challenging our sergeant at arms, Sledgehammer!"

The club erupted in cheers, and I noticed many of the bikers raising their drinks in my direction and yelling things like, "Nice knowing ya!" and "Hope your life insurance is paid up!"

I leaned in to yell in Belladonna's ear. "You are going to owe me *big time* after this is over."

She slapped me lightly on the cheek a few times and laughed. "C'mon, it'll be fun. When's the last time you had a decent brawl?" She paused and seemed to reconsider her words. "Never mind, forget what I just said. You only have to last three minutes anyway, so just try to stay out of his reach and pick your shots. The round will be over before you know it."

"I want you to know, if I hulk out and kill everyone in sight, I'm holding you accountable."

"Oh, suck it up, you big baby. This is going to be child's play for you."

By this time, several Pack members had bustled us over to a raised boxing ring that took up one side of the club. Sledgehammer walked in from the front entrance, peeling off his colors, jacket, and shirt underneath to reveal a chiseled torso that looked way out of place on a middle-aged biker. He was also one of the hairiest men I'd ever seen.

"You sure he hasn't already transformed?" I asked. Belladonna shook her head.

"It's against the rules. The rule is that if you're not Pack and you want an audience with the alpha, you have to fight one of the Pack. But, since you're human, he has to fight you in his human form."

"So I'm still dealing with a guy who stands at around six feet seven and weighs in at over three-hundred pounds, who can bench press a Harley and who heals like Wolverine. Great."

She slapped me again on the cheek, hard enough to sting. "Go get 'em, Tiger!"

I sighed and handed her my Craneskin Bag. "Don't lose this. It'll eventually find its way back to me, but it has a mind of its own and it's liable to let out all sorts of nasty stuff if I'm not around to keep it in its place."

She held it gingerly with two fingers. "Ugh, I hate sentient magical items. Make this quick."

I rolled my shoulders and neck out and leaned over to Sonny, who was busy taking bets. "What are the rules?"

He laughed. "Survive for three minutes. Or not—it doesn't matter. So long as you stay in the ring and don't run out, the fee is paid." He paused and cocked his head to one side. "You want me to place a bet for you?"

"What are the odds?"

"Five to one against you. Sorry, but it's the best I could do."

I thought about it for a moment and pulled out five twenties from my wallet, which was what remained of the paycheck I'd just cashed. "Put a hundred on me."

He chuckled and counted the money, tucking it away in his pants pocket. "I like your style, kid." Then he leaned in and spoke in my ear. "Don't hurt Sledge too bad, alright? You mess him up, and some of these wolves are going to take it out on you, Pack rules or no."

"Great, I'll keep that in mind," I said, cracking my neck with a grimace.

I grabbed the bottom rope, used it to pull me up to the canvas, and rolled under the bottom rope. I stood up just in time to hear the bell ring and to see Sledgehammer's massive fist coming right for the side of my head. Too late to slip or dodge the punch, I rolled with it, taking a glancing blow to the temple that made me see stars. I spun with the momentum, throwing a wild spinning kick that landed in his gut. I rolled away and stood on the other side of the ring, shaking off the effects of the punch and readying myself to weather this storm.

More like a hurricane, actually. Sledgehammer lived up to his name by leaping across the ring with a superman punch, which he followed with a flurry of punches delivered in a classic Western boxing style. Let me tell you, getting your ass kicked without losing your shit isn't the easiest thing to do. But I'd had a few years of practice, sparring with all the killers at Camelot. So I stayed on the move, mostly keeping out of his way while I determined the best tactics for dealing with his superior reach and size. Since he was all hands, and showed no inclination to kick or grapple, I decided to use that against him.

First, I waited for him to throw a jab with his lead hand again, and when he did I leaned back and delivered a sharp side kick to his knee, buckling it slightly and stopping his forward momentum. Rebounding from that kick, I dropped to the floor and spun, hooking that same knee with the back of my own and turning it sideways at an unnatural angle. I heard a "snap" as his knee twisted and he fell hard to the canvas. I felt bad about his knee, but he was a werewolf, after all; he'd heal in no time flat. Better him than me.

I had to give him credit, because he didn't grab his leg or show any other sign that his knee had blown. Sledge was tough, and he quickly got his good leg under him to get back to his feet. No way was I allowing that. I dove in for a single leg takedown, tucking my head under his arm as he pummeled my upper back and ribs with punches. Despite his superior strength, the blows were mostly weak and ineffective, because he had no base or leverage with me driving him back into the canvas. Soon I had him on his back, and after a brief scramble I ended up sitting high on his chest in the full mount, raining blows down on his face and head.

As I suspected, Sledgehammer was an old-school boxer, and not very skilled on the ground. However, he was very strong and could take a serious beating. Before I knew it, he'd grabbed me by the hips, eating punches the entire time as he threw me off him and into the ring ropes, a tremendous feat of strength considering his inferior position on the bottom.

I bounced off the ring ropes and landed on my feet, catching my balance just as Sledgehammer stood up. He was still a little wobbly on that left leg, and his face was battered and bleeding, but he was definitely game for continuing the fight. We both shuffled forward to close the gap when I heard a voice speak above the din and chaos at ringside. A hush fell over the crowd, and Sledge-hammer stopped his forward momentum mid-stride.

"Enough! The fee has been paid, and I need my people whole and in one piece. Sonny, send the Circle hunter and druid back to see me when you're finished with them."

Sonny nodded, and Sledgehammer dropped his hands to his sides. He nodded at me with respect. "Next time, druid."

"I'm not a—never mind. Sure, good fight. Sorry about the knee."

He grinned. "Don't be. That was the most fun I've had in months."

"Can't say the same, but I appreciate the sentiment."

The big 'thrope laughed and shook out his leg a few times, producing an audible "pop" on the third attempt. He shook my hand and left the ring with a slight limp, but I had no doubts that he'd be good as new within the hour.

I, on the other hand, didn't have near the recuperative abilities of a werewolf. Being a champion had its benefits, including aggression, improved reflexes, and being a bit stronger and faster than the average schmuck, but regeneration wasn't part of the package. In the past, I'd relied on druid potions and salves for increasing the speed at which I healed after a hard fight, but I hadn't had the need to brew any up in some time. I felt the side of my head where his fist had connected, and rubbed my hands up and down my battered and bruised arms, dreading how I was going to feel in the morning.

Once I was certain nothing was broken, I rolled out of the ring and walked over to Sonny. "I think you owe me some money."

He pulled a huge roll of bills out of his pocket and peeled off five hundreds. "Happy to pay it, kid. You just made me a fat stack of cash."

I took the cash and folded it up, stuffing it in the front pocket of my jeans. "Pleasure doing business with you."

He nodded. "Pleasure's all mine. Sledge is one tough son of a bitch. But I know what it means to be druid trained, so I was happy to take those bets." He tucked his roll of cash back in his pocket. "Now, let's get you back to see Samson."

FOURTEEN

Journal Entry—Nine Months, Six Days A.J.

Well, I finally met up with Belladonna again, but only after a couple of days of her hounding me with texts and phone calls. Honestly, I was happy hanging around with Jesse at home, catching her up on everything that had happened since... well, since I'd lost her. Mom knocked on my door a few times, saying she was worried about how much I was talking to myself. I figured it was best to keep her in the dark; she wasn't clued in, and her mind sort of blocked out anything weird by default.

A lot of mundanes were like that; their minds just chose to ignore any glimpse they might see of the supernatural world, the world beneath our own. It's what made it possible for even the weakest fae to conceal their true nature; all that most human minds needed was the slightest little push to keep them believing fairy tales weren't real, and myths were only that.

So instead, I told Mom I was just doing exercises that Dr. Larsen had assigned me, talking to Jesse as if she was really there. That seemed to satisfy her, although she kept checking in on me throughout the day. I fully expected her to call Dr. Larsen, and while I knew that doctor-patient confidentiality would keep my secret safe from Mom, it would also mean that I'd have to tell Dr. Larsen about Jesse.

Anyway, after a couple of days of staying in my room talking to Jesse, my mom told me that if that Donna girl kept calling, she was going to report her to the police for harassment. So I finally called Belladonna back, and she reacted with relief, then urgency. She insisted that I meet her immediately, so I agreed to drive into town the following morning to speak with her about whatever had her so riled.

The next day I met her for coffee at the same place as before, and she pulled out one of those old texts she'd borrowed, flipping it open to a passage that she'd marked with a sticky note. I snapped a picture of it and copied it by hand here:

"The typical haunting is usually nothing more than an echo of energy, a remnant of the deceased's thoughts, memories, and emotions, or in extreme instances the combined thoughts, memories, and emotions of a group of deceased individuals. These phenomena are harmless, akin to seeing the reflection of a moving car in a window. The reflection itself may appear real, but it has no inertial influence on the physical world.

"On the other hand, ghasts, ghosts, and spirits are sentient, fully cognizant supernatural creatures that for some reason or another are trapped on this plane of existence and unable to move on to the next. Often, this is due to a traumatic event that has psychologically damaged the spirit's "mind," if one could truly say a ghost has a mind in the traditional sense. Unfortunately, this results in the ghost or spirit being trapped on this plane until they experience a triggering event that allows them to complete their journey to the world beyond.

"Tragically, many such spirits are never able to move on to the next realm of existence, and due to the laws of conservation and entropy (which, dear reader, still govern supernatural entities and phenomena) they eventually fade from existence entirely. Research on such cases is limited, but it is theorized by the foremost parapsychologists in the field (namely Chatterjee and Jorgensen) that once an entity expends sufficient energy over time, they lose the ability to remain coherent. It is further theorized that in such cases the spirit's essence dissipates via a sort of cosmic diffusion, returning to the universe as heat, light, or sound energy, never to regain their previous cognizant, self-aware, autonomous state."

Obviously, this is not good. Something must be keeping Jesse on this side, preventing her from moving on to her eternal rest. What if I'm what's keeping her from leaving? What if she's only here because I'm a complete mess? And if so, how can I convince her that it's okay to move on?

I need to figure this out before I lose her for good. Better that I live a full, long life and rejoin her in the afterlife, than for me to have her spirit with me for a few months or years, only for her to fade away and become lost to oblivion.

Shit. It's like I'm killing her all over again. What am I going to do?

-McC

AUSTIN, Texas—Present Day

Sonny walked us back to his alpha's den, which was a room in the back of their clubhouse with a small bar, pool table, large poker table and chairs, and a whole mess of pin-up posters featuring women who sported a lot of ink and not a lot else. It smelled of stale cigar smoke, weed, spilled liquor, and testosterone. And sex, which to be honest was kind of gross.

There were dartboards on the walls, which were dotted with a variety of knives and other sharp toys. Along one wall an impromptu shooting range had been set up, complete with a mannequin that had been shot more times than Bonnie and Clyde's '34 Ford. The brick wall behind it was peppered with fractures and bullet holes. I figured they'd just brick it over when it completely started to crumble.

I gave the place a once over and whistled. "My compliments to your decorator."

Sonny chuckled. "You get enough wolves together in one place, and eventually you're going to end up with something that looks like this joint."

Belladonna blew a short puff of air from her nose. "Mid-century chauvinist—how charming. I thought you had more class than this, Colin."

That remark surprised me, coming from Bells. I'd known her for a long time, and she'd always presented herself as a brassy, sexually liberated woman who took what she wanted and to hell with what anyone thought. In fact, I more or less thought of her as one of the guys; that is, when she wasn't coming on to me. But the more I thought about it, the more it made sense—because if anyone was going to have feminist values, it was Belladonna Becerra.

"Don't assume I was talking about the posters, Bells." I winked at Sonny behind her back and nodded while pointing at a nearby poster. He nodded back to me in shared solidarity over the universal male appreciation of the female form.

Belladonna wasn't having it, and shook her head as we made our way through the room. "I saw that, Colin," she stated with just the slightest bit of displeasure in her voice. "Stop being a pig, it doesn't suit you. And besides, what would Jesse think?"

Belladonna always knew how to get me to behave. All she had to do was pull the Jesse card and I'd check myself in short order. "Sorry, Bells, I guess I just kind of think of you as one of the guys."

Sonny's eyes grew big as saucers, and he looked at me and shook his head ruefully. Belladonna glanced back and gave me a look that could curdle milk.

"Men," she huffed, crossing her arms and giving me the evil eye.

Sonny led us to the table in back, and gestured that we should take a seat. I had the presence of mind to wait for Belladonna to sit first, but I also had the common sense to resist pulling a chair out for her. I didn't remember it ever being this hard with Jesse; we just fit like a lock and key.

I got comfortable while Bells pointedly ignored my presence. Sonny patted me on the shoulder and whispered in my ear before walking away. "Samson likes you, so this should go well so long as you're respectful and listen to what he has to say. But as for the girl, well—you touch that hot stove enough, and eventually you'll learn how to stop when you're ahead."

Sonny nodded to Samson, who sat at the card table across from us, sipping a glass of whiskey and staring at nothing in particular. The table was lit by an overhead bulb, but he leaned back in his chair, just out of the circle of light made by the lampshade. Despite the shadows, I could make him out as he quietly sipped his liquor and stared off into a far corner of the room.

The Pack alpha was nothing much to look at; he was neither large, nor muscular, nor physically imposing in any way. I guessed his height at about five-foot-ten, his weight at about one hundred and seventy-five pounds, and noted that he was lean and wiry like a rodeo cowboy. He sported the thick, unruly facial hair that seemed to be popular with a lot of the Pack, but his head was clean shaven. He had tattoos on his long, chiseled forearms, and wore his colors on a leather vest, bare-chested, like he was daring you to say something about it. Yet he had a presence that was both intimidating and strangely comforting all at once, kind of like Chuck Norris. One look at the guy and you didn't know whether you wanted to fight him, run from him, or be his best friend.

I was leaning toward fighting him, at the moment. Just being around him was stirring something within me that I didn't want to let out, and I gripped the edge of the table in order to suppress the urge to jump across it at him.

He set his drink on the table, rocking forward so his face was clearly visible in the light. His ice blue eyes fixed me in place, shining with gold flecks as his rough baritone voice cut through the low thrum of Southern rock that drifted through the walls from next door.

"I can help you calm that beast inside. But you'd have to submit, and I don't think you're ready for that yet. Damned shame, because I can see how it's eating at you, day by day. You're gonna lose that battle, eventually, if you don't learn how to control it."

His voice cut through the rage building inside of me, and calmed me instantly. I shook my head and took a deep breath, relaxing as the Pack magic he exerted washed over me.

"Couldn't do that without having the Pack close by," he explained. "Figured it was better than having you wig out on me. Not that I wouldn't like to see how that turned out, but I have my Pack to consider. 'Sides, I need your cooperation if we're going to sort out this mess we're in."

"Thanks," I mumbled, still not sure whether I liked being subdued by Pack magic. At that moment, Sonny, Sledge, and a few other 'thropes burst into the room. Two of them had guns in hand, and Sledge carried a hammer that would have given Mjolnir a run for its money.

"You alright boss?" he asked with concern in his voice.

Samson raised a hand dismissively. "Appreciate the concern, boys, but it's alright. Just had a little disagreement between my beast and his. Nothing to be alarmed about."

Sledge fixed us with a look that said he didn't like it, and to watch it or he'd be back. "We'll be outside if you need us," he said as they left and closed the door.

Belladonna leaned on the table with both elbows and made eye contact with Samson, sparing me a glance that said I still wasn't out of the doghouse. Of course, I never knew there was a doghouse to begin with, but that didn't matter because I obviously didn't get a say.

"If you two are done," she stated coolly, "we have serious matters to discuss."

Samson laughed to himself and took a pull from his glass. He looked at me with sympathy. "What'd you do to piss her off? Never mind, none of my business."

He emptied his glass and addressed us both in turn. "Look, I know why you're here, and I know that the Circle and Maeve both probably think the Pack has been killing elves on fae land. But I'm here to tell you that it wasn't a wolf who killed those elves. It might look that way, but that's just because someone wants a war between the Pack and the Fae Court."

Belladonna's eyes were slits as she spoke. "I was told

by the Circle that the bites, marks, and wounds on those fae were conclusively made by a lycanthrope. I can't see any reason why my superiors would lie to me about such things. Our theory is that you have a rogue wolf in your Pack, or that there's an independent player, a lone wolf who is operating independent of your authority."

Samson stroked his beard and pursed his lips in thought. "Well, I have to admit that your theory sounds perfectly reasonable—except that's not the case. Pack bonds allow me to know what my Pack members are up to whenever they're in a heightened emotional state. Fear, shame, rage, love—these are all emotions that we feel through the Pack bonds."

"Must be a bitch to keep anything secret," I quipped.

He smirked. "You don't know the half of it. We don't have a lot of females in the Pack, which is just the way it shakes out. No one ever wants to turn a female, because the process is, well, violent. But when we have females around and two Pack members are involved, everyone knows it. It's why a lot of our Pack members end up mating with mundanes."

Belladonna leaned away from the table and shook her head slightly. "I'm just not buying it. I saw the bodies, and there are few creatures that would've savaged a body like that. It was a classic 'thrope attack, in each and every case."

The alpha drummed his fingers on the table, then

stood up suddenly. "Follow me. I'm going to show you something that few people know about, but if it helps convince you that we're not involved with those killings, I'll just have to take the risk that word doesn't get out."

I pushed away from the table and rose to follow him. "Why all the secrecy?"

He raised a hand dismissively. "You'll see. This way."

We followed him out a side door, down a hallway and into a kitchen area. In the kitchen, he pulled a trap door open and flipped a light switch nearby. A light came on below, illuminating a set of wooden stairs leading into a basement.

Samson gestured for us to enter. "After you."

Belladonna hesitated to enter, and I didn't blame her. Creepy basements topped my list of least favorite places to go in an enemy stronghold.

I looked at Samson and raised an eyebrow. "Seriously?"

He rubbed his forehead. "If I had wanted you two dead, I'd have had the Pack kill you before you ever got near me. But fine, I'll lead the way if it makes you feel any better." The wolf descended the stairs, and I followed him down with Belladonna on my heels.

The basement area looked to be used for food preparation as well as storage. Cases of beer and liquor lined the walls, stacked in neat rows, and the concrete floor was polished and spotless. A drain sat just a few feet from a stainless steel table that held a huge butcher block —and a collection of knives and other cutlery that would impress Dexter.

I pointed at the table and floor drain. "You're not doing much for my confidence here, you know."

He sighed. "We're lycanthropes—we eat a lot of pork and beef. I have to buy it in bulk straight from the ranchers who raise them, else we'd go broke in no time. There's only so much meth you can run without getting caught, you know."

I tilted my head and shrugged slightly. "At least you're honest."

Samson walked over to a large stainless steel door and pulled it open. Inside was a walk-in cooler with sides of beef and pork hanging from steel butcher's hooks, just as he'd said. The fog cleared from the room, revealing three frozen, headless, and very dead were-wolves. All three bodies were propped against the back wall in a neat furry row.

FIFTEEN

Journal Entry—9 Months, 9 Days A.J.

I met Belladonna at the coffee shop today, and it turns out that she's been doing more digging in the Circle archives. She says we need to find a way to communicate with Jesse so we can find out what she wants or needs, and convince her to move on. I told her that I've been talking to Jesse nonstop, and that nothing I say seems to make the slightest difference; I still feel her presence at my house, just like before.

Belladonna said that from what she's read in the archives, if we don't figure out a way to clearly communicate with Jesse, then we might never be able to help her leave this plane of existence. She'll be trapped here until she fades away into nothing. I can't accept that, but neither I nor Belladonna know how to speak with the dead.

But, I know someone who does. And even though I swore I'd never have anything to do with him again, it looks like I'm going to need Finn's help to fix this mess.

My only worry is that I'll go apeshit on him and kill him before he can help us speak to Jesse's ghost.

-McC

AUSTIN, Texas—Present Day

Belladonna was the first to comment. "Holy shit, what happened to them?"

Samson tongued a molar and tsked. "Far as we can tell, they were paralyzed by a magical spell of some sort and decapitated. None of the bodies show any sign of a major struggle, and we all know that werewolves don't go down easy. The only problem with that theory is, none of them smell like magic."

That was interesting, but not unusual. Most magical spells left a sort of scent or imprint on the recipient. And if you were familiar with a particular magic user's signature, you could easily identify them by detecting that scent or imprint. Which was why a lot of magic users who plied their trade on the wrong side of the law learned how to remove traces of their magic from their victims.

"Do you mind if I examine them?" I asked.

Samson nodded. "Help yourself, just be respectful.

Once we fully recover the bodies, we'll need to give them a proper burial."

For weres and other supernatural creatures, that often meant a funeral pyre. It was common knowledge that curses could be worked by gathering hair or other DNA from the victim. Superstition and myth said that one could be cursed that way, even in the afterlife. Also, many creatures were concerned about being brought back from the dead by a necromancer. But in modern times, it was suspected that the government was experimenting on supernatural creatures in an attempt to control or weaponize them. None of the powers that be among the supernatural species were interested in contributing to that cause, so most had taken to burning their dead.

I walked into the cooler and used my second sight to examine the corpses. Just as Samson had claimed, they were devoid of all traces of magic, save for the remnants of their own innate werewolf magic. Seeing nothing of interest, I used my mundane vision to examine them for less obvious wounds, the kind that might have been missed by someone not familiar with investigative techniques.

Being druid-trained, I'd been taught by Finnegas how to identify signs of poisoning, trauma, magic, and other common causes of death among both supernatural and mundane creatures. But these 'thropes showed no signs of struggle, and they bore no hidden wounds that might have contributed to their demise. They didn't smell of poison, either, although I assumed that Samson would have mentioned it if they had. The cause of death was obvious, but how the killer or killers managed to behead three full-grown and transformed werewolves without a scuffle pointed to only one possibility: magic. Powerful magic.

Belladonna had joined me inside the cooler and examined one of the other weres. "Whoever did this was a first-rate magic user. Weres are naturally resistant to magic, and tend to shake off most paralysis spells pretty quickly."

"Even for a strong magic user, it would've taken a lot of juice to hold one of these 'thropes while their accomplice dealt the finishing blow. And look at these cuts—there are no jagged edges. Whoever finished these 'thropes off must've been using a +5 vorpal sword to make cuts this clean."

Bells punched my shoulder, a little harder than what might be considered playful. "You are such a nerd."

I raised my hand. "Guilty, as charged."

I walked out of the cooler and found Samson sitting on the steel table. "You think the fae did this?"

He sniffed and made an almost imperceptible shake of his head. "My instincts tell me that's what happened, that these wolves were taken out by a fae hit squad as payback for losing their own. But my gut tells me that this was only made to look like it was done by fae."

Belladonna strode out of the cooler, shutting the door behind her. "You think it's all a set up."

The alpha clucked his tongue. "Don't you?"

Belladonna crossed her arms and barked a short laugh. "I don't like it, if that's what you're asking. But I'm still not convinced that this isn't a turf war between you and Maeve."

I sighed. "C'mon, Bells, seriously? What benefit would that be for the Pack? Maeve's power base and interests are in keeping the fae hidden from humans, and exerting power and influence behind the scenes. They get their jollies from swapping human babies with doppelgängers, taking humans Underhill to be used as slaves, and using sexual magic to seduce and then slowly kill human men and women. Samson and his Pack make their money in vice, plain and simple. Neither side has anything the other wants."

She ran her fingers through her long, thick hair and hissed. "But it doesn't make any sense. Who'd want to pit Maeve against the wolves?"

Samson stood up. "I know my opinion means shit here, because I obviously have a vested interest in clearing the Pack's rep. But if you ask me, a tussle between the fae and the Pack would be the perfect distraction, to keep the Circle and everyone else occupied while something big was going down."

"It's a possibility," I said. "Who else knows about—" I nodded toward the cooler "—them?"

"Outside of this room? Just Sledge and two other enforcers. And they know how to keep their muzzles shut. If word of this got out, the Pack would demand that we go to war with the fae. So we're keeping it under wraps, just until we figure out who murdered our Pack members. But I already have 'thropes asking questions about the missing wolves, and starting to get suspicious."

Belladonna's eyes narrowed as she addressed the alpha. "I'll keep this quiet as long as I can. Just know that the Circle is going to keep investigating the Pack for these murders. And if I can't bring them a suspect within a day or two, my superiors are likely to assume that you're protecting the guilty party."

Samson laughed without smiling. "If I can't figure out who's behind this in a day or so, word is going to get out. And if that happens, we're going to have an all-out war on our hands. The Circle will be the least of the Pack's problems."

I extended my hand to the alpha. "Thanks for your time and cooperation, Samson. I give you my word that I'll let you know what I find out. I doubt Maeve's behind any of this, and if that's the case she's aware that it's not the wolves killing her people."

He shrugged. "Like I said, once this gets out the Pack'll be crying for blood. And alpha or no, if the Pack wants to go to war there's not much I can do to change their minds."

WE LEFT the clubhouse and Belladonna dropped me off at the junkyard. She didn't have much to say before leaving, other than to keep her posted if I found out anything. I figured she was still mad about what I'd said earlier, but I was too tired to try to fix it. Not that I didn't want to—it's just that I knew in the state I was in, I'd only make it worse.

Finn was waiting for me on the warehouse dock when I walked into the yard. The dogs were hanging out with him, and he was scratching behind one dog's ear and giving the other one a belly rub. Like I said, most animals were suckers for druids—at least, those who weren't cursed.

My shoulders slumped, because I didn't feel like dealing with him at the moment. It was late, and I just wanted to go to bed so I could get some rest before I had to go kappa hunting in a few hours with that idiot from CIRCE. I waved Finn off and walked past him.

"Finn, I don't have any money to loan you, and I'm not telling Maureen to increase your allowance. If you want more money, you'll just have to stay clean and earn it here in the yard working for Ed."

He looked down at the dogs briefly, and they both perked up and moved away so he could stand up. It was eerie how he could communicate with some animals without using verbal commands or even hand signals. It was almost like a form of animal telepathy, but he said it was just being in tune with the animal's energy. These days that sounded like a crock of horse shit to me, but then again since Jesse had died I was biased against much of what Finn had told me in the past.

"That's not what I wanted to talk to you about."

I rubbed my face. "Can it wait till morning? Because I have to be somewhere in—" I paused to look at my phone "—about five hours, and I need to get some sleep before then."

His shoulders sagged a little, making me feel sorry for him, but not nearly enough to show it. "I just wanted to tell you that I'm going to get clean."

"You've said that before. I'll believe it when I see it."

He stood up and approached me. "This time, I mean it. I had a vision, Colin, and you're about to face something that might be worse than the Caoránach. When the time comes, you're going to need my help."

"Oh brother, I've heard that line before. Look, if this is just another ploy to regain my trust so you can manipulate me into enabling you, forget it—"

"Damn it, boy, listen to me!" he exclaimed as he stamped his foot on the dock and pulled himself to his full height.

I smelled ozone and felt the ground shake slightly beneath us as the dogs scattered. For a brief instant, I saw a glimpse of the powerful druid who'd mentored me through my youth and into manhood. Even in the weak moonlight, I could see that his eyes were clear and free from their customary drug-induced glaze. Then he staggered a little; his brief display of power had taken a lot out of him.

"Listen to me, please," he wheezed, reaching out to the wall for support.

"You're drunk, Finn. Go sleep it off, alright?" I knew he wasn't, but I didn't want to deal with him and I needed an excuse to end the conversation. I walked off toward the warehouse entrance. Finnegas called out after me in a weak, raspy voice.

"You're going to need my help, damn it! And like it or not, you'll have it when the time comes. Mark my words: something is coming, and you can't fight it alone."

I waved over my shoulder without looking back. "'Something is coming'—yeah, that's not nebulous at all. Whatever, old man. I'm going to bed now."

I barely heard his last words as he whispered them to the dark. "At least, you can't fight it alone and remain human," he said, voice quivering.

I gently shut and locked the door behind me and sagged against the wall for a moment, taking time to touch a kiss to Jesse's photo. Then I kicked off my shoes, stumbled the last few feet, and flopped face first into bed.

"Tell it to someone who cares," I mumbled as I drifted off to sleep.

SIXTEEN

Journal Entry—9 Months, 12 Days A.J.

Well, that went well. I found Finn at his offices, drunk as a skunk. His secretary Maureen says he's pretty much been that way since the night it happened. I ended up in a shouting match with a drunken druid; thankfully it didn't come to blows. We're trying to get him sobered up long enough so he can tell me how to fix this.

Wouldn't be surprised if he lets us down again, though. In fact, I'll only be shocked if he actually comes through for us. Guess we'll see.

-McC

AUSTIN, Texas—Present Day

An alarm on my phone woke me up the next morning, and I reached over to shut it off before it vibrated off my footlocker. I had a moment of panic thinking I might have lost my cash, and frantically patted my pockets down until I located the small wad of bills Sonny had given me. I rolled onto my back, hanging one leg off the bed and staring at the ceiling, wondering if I could afford to buy an espresso machine for my room with the money I'd made.

Sighing with relief, I sat up and wiped the sleep from my eyes, then grabbed my shaving kit and walked down to the public restroom to clean up before I headed over to CIRCE. Taking a whiff of my pits on the way there, I decided it was worth risking being caught in the buff by the early crew to get a decent shower before I headed out. No one was in the yard or warehouse yet, and I still had a few minutes until the morning shift arrived. I ducked back in my room for a towel and headed behind the warehouse to take a freezing cold shower.

The shower stall I'd rigged up was nothing more than some metal uprights, a wooden pallet for a shower floor, and a few pieces of corrugated metal left over from the last time Ed repaired the fence. To say it was drafty would have been an understatement, but short of using the student rec on campus it was my only option for getting my Irish Spring on. Besides, part of my training had involved spending days on end in the deep woods with Jesse, with little more than a knife and the clothes on our backs to keep us alive. So I was used to bathing in streams and creeks, making this a luxury compared to what I'd gone through to become druid-trained.

By this time, I was late for my meeting with Elias, so I had to skip my usual stop at La Crème. The good news was that the cold water woke me up a bit, and I decided to forego my helmet on the ride over to get the full effect. That proved to be a mistake. The cool morning air left me feeling chilled and miserable by the time I reached CIRCE's offices.

Numbed and tired, I pulled my scooter around back, where I almost collided with a ruby red Porsche four-door that was leaving as I turned in the drive. I honked my horn and someone flipped me off in reply out of the dark, tinted windows. I returned the favor and pulled up to the back entrance to find Elias loading the panel van with gear.

"Hey, Colin—glad you're here! Help me load this stuff up, and we'll be ready to tackle your first trip into the field."

I planted a fake smile on my face, and tried to sound as enthusiastic as possible. "Morning, Elias. Sure, happy to help."

I grabbed a large black equipment case and placed it in the van, making an effort to chat as we worked. I decided to play dumb, just to see how reliable Elias would be with regard to his knowledge of the supernatural. "I'm—excited about what we'll find out there today. But just what is a 'kappa'?"

He took the metal shipping container I handed him, and thought for a moment before answering. "Well, a kappa is a Japanese water sprite. Legend has it that they can be either benevolent or cruel to people—it all depends on their mood and so on."

"But what do they look like? They must be pretty big to be able to eat a whole cow."

He laughed and shook his head. "Naw, they're little guys. Maybe four feet tall, and they look like a cross between a monkey, a frog, and a turtle. Sort of like ninja turtles, to be honest, and kind of cute in a way. Are they dangerous? Yeah, but there's nothing for you to worry about, so long as you watch yourself and follow my lead."

Elias was either stupid, or he was purposely playing down how deadly kappa could be. Strictly speaking, kappa were yōkai, demons that were more or less the Japanese equivalent of the unseelie fae from European legend. They were strong, *much* stronger than a human, with lots of sharp teeth and claws to match. Kappa were quick and violent, and when hungry they'd attack and eat a human without hesitation. In fact, it was a wonder that this rancher Mr. Graves hadn't been eaten already.

At that moment, I decided that Elias was not my favorite person. I had the distinct impression that he cared little about the safety of his staff, and was only interested in capturing the creatures CIRCE supposedly relocated. That indicated he was in it for more than just pure altruism, and I began to wonder whether someone might be paying him for the creatures CIRCE captured. If so, I needed to find out who that was, and what their motivations were for doing so. Then, hopefully, that would lead me to the Tathlum.

The ride to the ranch was long and boring, and Elias listened to early 70s pop the entire way. It was kind of like going on a road trip with Ed. Ed was a bit older than my mom, and he was into the same style of music. KC and the Sunshine Band, Earth Wind and Fire, stuff like that. It wasn't bad music for the most part, but Elias sang along with just about every song. By the time we arrived at the ranch ninety minutes later, I had a headache and seriously wanted to shoot him in the face with a tranq gun, in the worst way possible.

Mr. Graves met us at the gate, and we followed his beat up work truck for a mile or so. Eventually we reached a creek that had been dammed to create a small pond surrounded by live oaks and willow trees. Combined with the beautiful fall weather we were having it was all very picturesque. If it hadn't been for the half-eaten cattle carcasses strewn along the edge of the watering hole and the smell of rotten flesh, I'd have been tempted to go in for a dip. We parked about fifty meters away and got out of the van, waiting for Mr.

Graves to join us. Instead, he waved at us and leaned over to roll down the window.

"Aw hell, I'm not getting out. Damn near got eaten yesterday—those little bastards are quick. Naw, I'll let you city folk handle it, and come back to haul them carcasses out of the water once you give the all clear."

I decided to gather some intel, just in case Elias was too stupid to ask the right questions before the old man left us to our work. "Mr. Graves, if you don't mind me asking, how many of them have you seen?"

He scratched his nose and shrugged. "Hard to say. I reckon there's at least three of them moving around down there. Usually if one comes out of the water the others stay under and watch, kind of like gators with their eyes peeking out just above the surface. And with the way their heads are shaped, you almost can't see 'em when they're submerged like that."

That physical feature Mr. Graves was referring to was a unique characteristic of kappa. In lieu of a brain, they had a weird concave indentation on their heads that held water like a bowl. That was their greatest weakness, because somehow the water in a kappa's skull deforma-tion acted as part of their central nervous system. Once out of the water, if you could somehow get them to spill the contents of their skull cup, they were helpless.

When Mr. Graves mentioned seeing more than one kappa, Elias' face blanched. It appeared that he hadn't expected to deal with more than one or two of these creatures. I wasn't overly concerned about it, because I had a surprise tucked away inside my Craneskin Bag. Still, the plan I had in mind both for dealing with the kappa and getting some answers out of Elias might be tricky if there were more than three of the little bastards lurking in that pond.

Elias covered his nervousness well, I had to give him that. He cleared his throat and gave Mr. Graves a reassuring nod. "Don't you worry, we'll have these little guys off your land and safely in another habitat before you know it."

I raised a hand to catch the old man's attention. "Sir, you seem awful calm about having monsters on your property. Is this the first time this has happened?"

Mr. Graves pushed the brim of his straw cowboy hat back on his head and scratched at his hairline. "Saw a bigfoot once. It got up real close, sniffing around and stuff, and scared the living tar out of me. Since then, I figure there's more to this world than most people know about. Which brings me to ask—it's just you two boys catching these things? Ain't no others from your outfit comin'?"

Elias nodded. "Just us, but we can handle it."

The rancher shrugged. "Well, it's your funeral. I'll check back on you around lunch, and call your office if you get eaten." He then put his truck in gear and cut a quick U-turn in the clearing, driving faster than was probably safe back the way we came. I watched him go and then turned to Elias.

"What now? I mean, you're the expert—I'm just here to watch and learn from your *extensive* experience."

Elias looked toward the pond and stammered slightly, apparently at a loss as to how to capture three or perhaps four kappa at once without being eaten.

"Yes—of course, of course. Start pulling those traps out, and set them up close to the water line. But not too close—I don't want you to become a casualty of the cause on your very first day."

He continued staring at the water, tapping a finger on his chin and conveniently becoming occupied with deep thoughts while I did all the heavy work. I sighed quietly and did what he asked, keeping one eye on the water line as I dragged the heavy cage traps close to the shore. I spotted at least two sets of eyes hanging back from the water's edge, and a third skimming under the surface toward me as I set up the second trap.

Without bait, it was unlikely any of the kappa would be dumb enough to enter the traps. But Elias hadn't instructed me to place anything inside the traps to lure the kappa in. I had come prepared, however, and surreptitiously reached inside my Craneskin Bag, pulling out a few Japanese cucumbers I'd picked up from a farmer's market years ago and stowed away for just such an occasion. Thanks to the temporal stasis field inside the bag, they were as fresh as the day I'd bought them. I cut them in two with my pocket knife and tossed several in each of the cages, backing away quickly while still keeping an eye on the water.

Sure enough, the two that had been hanging back emerged as I retreated, the water in their skull cups sloshing back and forth without spilling a drop as they walked onto dry land. Cucumbers were a favorite food of kappa, only second to small children, and I knew they'd be hard-pressed to resist the Japanese variety as they were difficult to come by here in the States. Each of them marched straight into the traps, stepping on the trigger plates as they gobbled the cucumber halves up greedily. The gates to each cage slammed down behind them, latching and trapping them inside. The kappa keened and wailed when they realized they'd been fooled, beating on the side of the cages with their webbed and clawed hands.

Elias clapped his hands together as I approached, walking backward so I could keep an eye on the remaining kappa.

"You see, Colin? I told you this would be an easy first job. Just look at those shells, and their beaked mouths— fine specimens, fine indeed." His man bun bobbed up and down as he spoke excitedly and marched down to the traps.

I decided not to warn him, since I needed him good and frightened and in no position to negotiate. He was hiding something, and short of beating it out of him I didn't see any convenient way to get him to reveal what CIRCE's connection with Ananda Corp was, or why they were footing the bill for CIRCE's operations. Instead, I reached into the van and grabbed one of the cases, opening it while he was preoccupied with the caged kappa. Then, I followed at a safe distance and observed as he circled each of the cages in turn.

As he rounded the first cage, the final kappa's creepy frog eyes began to glide through the water, closer and closer to the shore. The cages were a good twenty feet from the water's edge, but I knew that once on shore, the creature could clear that in a heartbeat. As Elias yammered on, he turned his back to the water a second time—and that's when the creature struck.

In the blink of an eye it leapt from the water like a dolphin clearing a wave, landing on the shore just ten feet from Elias, who startled and froze like a deer in headlights. As the kappa closed the gap between them, I waited for just the right moment before I triggered the net cannon I'd grabbed just moments before. The capture net flew forward at tremendous speed, entangling them just a few feet apart while taking them both down at once.

Elias began screaming as the kappa began clawing

and chewing at the net. "Oh shit, oh shit, oh shit—get me out of here before that thing frees itself. Quick, Colin, cut me loose and shoot it with a tranquilizer or something!"

I dropped the net cannon and sauntered up to them, taking my time about it and watching as the kappa tore the netting to shreds with its teeth and claws. I estimated that it'd be free within a minute or two, which gave me just enough time to have a lively chat with Elias.

I squatted down next to him and cleared my throat. "Well now, it looks like you're in quite a pickle. If my guess is right, that kappa is going to be free in, oh, maybe ninety seconds. But you—you're tangled up something fierce. I bet he'll be on you, just as soon as he gets loose."

He tugged at the net and looked at me through the holes in the webbing with a mixture of fear and desperation. "Colin, listen to me—that thing really will eat me if you don't get me out of here. Look, you want a paid position? Fine, just cut me loose, now!"

"Oh, this isn't about money, Elias. And I'm well aware of the danger you're in right now. I may be young, but I've dealt with a few kappa in my time, back while I was being trained as a hunter."

Elias did a double-take. "You were a hunter? You? Look, I don't know what kind of game you're playing, or who you're working for, but this is serious, Colin! You have to cut me out of here, and right now before that thing gets free."

His eyes darted back and forth between the creature and me; clearly he was thoroughly confused and frightened. *Perfect.*

"I'll get you out," I replied. "But not before I get some answers. Tell me what you know about the Tathlum."

"Tathlum? What the heck is a tathlum? I don't have any idea what you're talking about."

There was a loud ripping noise just at that moment, and one blue-green clawed arm thrust up through the net just a few feet away. "Time's running out, Elias. I'd start talking if I were you."

He cringed and tried to move away from the kappa, to no avail. "Okay, okay! I'll tell you what I know. Ananda Corp hired me last year to put this group together, said I could make a whole lot of money capturing rare animals. I was working for a rescue zoo at the time, making hardly enough to get by. I have a graduate degree, for Christ's sake! With the money they offered me, I jumped at the opportunity.

"I didn't know anything about, you know—" he looked over at the kappa, which now had its arm and shoulder through the net "—*them*, before I took the job. But after that first capture the pay was so good, I couldn't tell the people from Ananda no."

"And what are they doing with the creatures?"

Elias glanced over at the kappa again, which was doing its damnedest to wriggle out of the hole it'd made in the net. The creature kept looking at the helpless man beside him while licking its lips, muttering in Japanese all the while. I didn't speak much Japanese, but I caught the words for "eat" and "hungry" a few times. Elias made a little whining noise in the back of his throat and attempted to squirm away.

"Gah! They're taking them and torturing them, man. Asking them questions about artifacts, objects of power —forcing them to reveal whatever they know about mythical weapons and objects and whatnot. I think Ananda Corp is either dealing in them, or someone behind the scenes is a collector. Usually they interrogate the creatures at a farmhouse outside of town. It's where they have me make all my deliveries, once we've captured them."

"I'm going to need directions to that farm, Elias." I made a show of cleaning my fingernails and buffing them on my shirt. "But I haven't got all day—or rather, *you* don't have all day."

There was a loud ripping sound, and the kappa's head burst through the net. It began wriggling free in earnest, and would be clear within seconds. Elias yelped and tried to squirm away again, and a wet stain appeared on the front of his tan safari shorts.

"It's programmed into my phone's GPS! Here, take it!" He pulled a phone out of his pocket and shoved it through the netting. I grabbed it and pulled up his GPS app, finding it among his saved locations.

"Hey, this is out near Barton Hills Farm—I used to go to the corn maze out there when I was a kid. Huh." I stuck the phone in my pocket and began to walk off.

"Wait! Don't leave me here. Colin, you promised, man!" At that moment the kappa tore free from the net and stood up, looking back and forth from me to the easier prey still caught in the net. After a brief deliberation the creature's eyes locked on Elias', who began crying hysterically.

I shook my head. "Alright, you big baby," I exclaimed. I pulled out another cucumber from my bag, tearing it in two pieces and waving it around to get the kappa's attention.

Just as it turned its eyes toward me, I made my move, bowing deeply from the waist at a ninety-degree angle. I kept my eyes on the ground while holding my bow, and was soon rewarded by a splashing sound. I looked up and saw that the kappa, honor bound to return my show of respect, had spilled the contents of his skull cup on the ground before him. Drool ran freely from his beaked mouth, and he swayed drunkenly on his feet at half-mast.

Elias looked over at me and back at the kappa.

"What, that's it? That's all I had to do to capture these stupid things?"

"Yep. Once they spill that water from their heads, they're basically brain dead until someone refills their skull cup."

He shook his head and swore. "So, you're going to get me out of this net, right?"

"Nah, I think you can handle it." I began walking back to the van. Elias yelled after me as I departed.

"These Ananda people, they're bad news, you know. They'll kill you once they find out you're onto them. And I hope they do, you little shit!"

I hollered back over my shoulder. "So I guess that means I don't get the internship?"

SEVENTEEN

Journal Entry—9 Months, 14 Days A.J.

Maureen has managed to keep Finn away from the liquor store for twenty-four hours. She called and said he's in withdrawal, so we'd better come over quick because it's not safe to make someone his age go cold turkey.

Right. He's practically immortal; that's what two millennia of magic use will do to you. It actually kind of cheers me up to think that he's still vulnerable to a nasty hangover, though. I know I'm being petty, but the man ruined my life. It's going to be hard to face him when he's sober.

I guess I'd better head over before he crawls back in the bottle again.

-McC

. . .

AUSTIN, Texas—Present Day

Margie was nowhere to be found when I got back to CIRCE's offices. The SUV was also missing, so I assumed she was on her way to pick up Elias from Mr. Graves' ranch. I wouldn't lie and say that I didn't borrow a few things from CIRCE before leaving the van back at their offices; I figured they were ill-gotten goods, and therefore free for the taking. They had some pretty neat toys, and frankly I thought some of it might come in handy before this Maeve gig was finished. I snagged a few goodies, whatever I could fit through the opening of my Craneskin Bag, and left the keys to the van on Elias' desk.

With that unpleasant task out of the way, I went home and took a nap. When I woke I cleaned up and changed clothes, then sent Sabine a text telling her to meet me at Luther's place. It was about four o'clock in the afternoon when I left the junkyard, cruising up Congress on the Vespa with dreams of cold, strong coffee and a warm panini dancing in my head.

I checked my phone when I pulled into the alley behind La Crème, being sure to scan the shadows just in case Crowley was waiting to ambush me again. Sabine still hadn't returned my text, which was weird; she always texted me back right away. *Maybe her phone died. She's probably waiting for me in the cafe,* I thought.

With my stomach growling, I headed inside and

found Luther working the counter as usual. Most older vamps slept less and could handle being active during daylight hours. With so much time on his hands, I think he preferred hanging out at La Crème because it kept him busy. He waved me over as I walked in from the back of the cafe.

He looked concerned. "The garden gnome mafia left a message for you, maybe a couple of hours ago. Hope you're not doing business with those clowns."

I shook my head as I grabbed the envelope from him and tucked it inside my jacket. "Not on your second life. You seen Sabine today?"

He shook his head. "Nope. When she didn't stop in for her morning latte, I figured she was with you. You want your usual?"

I nodded. "And a roast beef and provolone sammich, if you don't mind. I'll be in back. If she comes in, tell her I'm here, okay?"

"You got it, stud." I glanced around again on the odd chance we both might have missed her, and turned back a second later as he was handing me my cold brew. Vampire speed was damned spooky sometimes.

After waiting for my sandwich, I munched it on my way to the back room. I grabbed a chair and pulled out my laptop to check my email, just in case Sabine had decided to go retro on me. No messages there, either. I called and left her a voicemail, then pulled out the envelope the dwarves had left.

Of course, it had been made by cutting and pasting individual letters that had been clipped from assorted magazines and newspapers. Duh, I already knew who left it. *Losers.*

The note read:

"WE hAv tHE glAIsTiG. BAck oF oR ShE dYes.

p.S. – tEll ThE oLD MaN hE sTiL oWeS uS."

My hands started shaking as I finished reading the note. "Oh, you weaselly little cock-juggling ass bandits—it is *on*," I muttered as I crumpled the note and tossed it on the table in front of me.

All things considered, I had to give them points for spelling glaistig properly. But the fact was, red caps didn't normally deal in kidnappings, at least not for money or leverage; they tended to eat the people they abducted. Besides, they mostly were concerned with keeping their drug money flowing, and shaking down any of the weaker fae who fell for their stupid protection racket.

No, this pointed to someone working behind the scenes. Somebody hired the dwarves to kidnap Sabine, either to distract me or to scare me off of whatever I'd stumbled on at CIRCE. Chances were good that Elias reported directly to someone at Ananda Corp, and he'd probably called them as soon as Margie showed up at Mr. Graves' place.

Shoulda' let that kappa eat him, I thought. I squeezed my hand into a fist so hard my knuckles cracked.

Suddenly I realized that I'd made a serious miscalculation with regards to how ruthless my unknown adversaries were, and just how far they'd go to keep me from getting to the bottom of the whole screwed up mess I'd stumbled into. Right now, my next step was finding Rocko and his crew so I could squeeze them for every bit of info they had, including who hired them and whether they were connected to this mysterious Ananda Corp and Maeve's missing magic rock.

Unfortunately, red caps were known to be mentally unstable and bloodthirsty as hell. And the longer they held Sabine, the greater the risk to her life—regardless of what they'd been tasked to do by whoever hired them. If I didn't find the little bastards, and soon, it was quite possible they'd kill Sabine out of sheer boredom and eat the evidence just to cover their tracks.

Only one person I knew could reliably lead me to their hide out. And as much as I hated asking Finn for help, he'd be sure to know where to find them. I chugged the rest of my coffee, grabbed my bag, and ran out the back door, thinking of all the hurt I was going to put on those little sociopaths, just as soon as I got my hands on them.

IT WAS after seven o'clock when I got back to the junk-yard, because five o'clock traffic in Austin was a bitch to drive in, even though I was splitting lanes the entire way. By the time I arrived, Ed had already closed up shop and headed home, deciding years before that he preferred working banker's hours and that the trickle of customers who came in after five o'clock simply weren't worth the effort. I unlocked the gate and pushed my scooter inside, and nearly had it closed when a small Toyota beater pulled up, blinding me with its headlights.

I waved them away. "We're closed!" I yelled.

I saw the silhouette of a large man's head poke out from the driver's side window. "Hey, Colin—check out my new wheels, yeah? Got it off some boy racer who was doing the ton and got stopped by some plod. His parents made him sell it, 'cuz he was skint and couldn't pay his fines. His loss, my gain, yeah?"

I held my hand up to block the headlights from shining in my eyes. "Hemi, is that you?"

"'Course it's me, you silly yank. Came to take you up on your offer to show me around town."

"How'd you find me?" I yelled over the sound of the

little four-banger's engine and exhaust as he revved it up.

"Nice, right?" he hollered back.

Sighing, I pushed my scooter out of the way and opened the gate so he could park. I needed to get rid of him, and fast, and there was no way I could do that while we were yelling at each other over all the racket his new tuner made. Hemi pulled his car in and parked it, then he hopped out and walked around the car, admiring his new ride.

"Got a small ding from a prang the kid got in, but nothing a little work can't fix right up." His face beamed as he showed his car off to me. "Hop in, we'll go for a strop."

I had to admit, it was a pretty cool car, a seventh-generation Celica that had been dropped and kitted out with some nice rims and wheels, custom exhaust, a carbon-fiber hood, and a body kit that gave it a much more aggressive look. It had been painted flat black and looked like it could run. On any other day, I'd be geeking out over it; right now, though, I had to find Sabine.

"Hemi, man, I'd love to hang out with you, but just not tonight. Something important came up, and I have to go help a friend."

He perked up and cocked an eyebrow, an expression that made him look exactly like the Rock. "Colin, you got someone who needs smashed, you just point me at 'em, yeah? We'll take care of 'em, then go get pissed after. A perfect night out!"

As much as I wouldn't mind having the big Maori on my side, I didn't want to drag him into my mess. "Hemi, my man, as much as I appreciate the offer, I—"

Just at that moment, something slammed into the wards and seals on the front gate of the junkyard with a tremendous crash, sending showers of sparks and arcs of blue light twenty feet above the fence line.

Hemi dropped into a crouch, reaching behind his back and leaving his hand there. "Oy, mate, what the hell was that?"

BOOM! Whatever it was slammed into the front gate again. I shifted my eyes into the supernatural spectrum, and saw that my wards and seals were straining under the force of whatever was trying to get inside the yard. I quickly vaulted on the hood of Ed's work truck nearby, climbing on the roof to get a look over the fence. From that vantage point, I saw a headless figure astride a horse on the other side of the gate, and he was swinging a huge battle axe at my wards.

I waved frantically at the Maori and pointed toward the other side of the junkyard.

"Hemi, this thing outside—it's dangerous. I don't have time to explain, but you have to get out of here, now. Drive around to the back of the yard and you'll see another gate. Once you're out keep going, and don't stop for anything."

He looked at me and scowled. "You want me to run? *Pfft*. Maori warriors don't run from nothing. Besides, we shed blood together, you and I. You may as well be part of my *hapu* now, yeah? Let's not piss around about it. I'm not going anywhere."

Without waiting for a response, the big man turned and locked his eyes on the gate while pulling a glowing greenstone *mere* from behind his back. The *mere* was a small, flat club with a lanyard on the handle, used by the Maori much like the Okinawan people used the nunchaku. The fence shook with an impact again, and in response Hemi began making frightening faces, sticking his tongue out and chanting while stomping out a *haka*, a war dance Maoris used to invoke their god of war.

With every lyrical chant, stomp, and slap, his weapon and tattoos seemed to glow a little brighter. *Well I'll be damned*, I thought to myself. *He's warding himself for battle.*

I shrugged and decided I'd better be ready for the Dullahan as well, and went over to the corner posts that held up the roof over the warehouse dock. They were made of iron; I'd engraved them with magic wards and symbols, and had been shoring it up on a weekly basis for months now. I touched them each in turn to activate them and the symbols began to shine a bright yellow, glowing and fading with the rhythm of the Dullahan's attacks on the gate. He was going to be in for quite a surprise when he broke through.

I didn't have time to get my hunting gear out of my room and put it on, but I did have a moment to reach into my Craneskin Bag and pull out the only weapon I trusted myself to wield. It was a spear, roughly seven feet long, wrapped in leather at the balance point of the shaft, lightly carved with runes down its length, and shod with silver at the butt and haft. The spearhead itself was nothing to look at; leaf-shaped and roughly a foot long, it gleamed dully as the razor-sharp edge caught the lamplight of the yard.

But the spear was deadly to mortals, and an effective weapon against most supernatural creatures and fae as well. I'd made it myself, with a little help from a leprechaun who'd owed me a favor. I could wield this weapon at a distance, and doing so would keep me out of the fray. In that manner I hoped I could avoid being driven to madness, thereby preventing a dangerous transformation and keeping my *ríastrad* at bay.

I hefted my spear and looked over at Hemi, just as he was finishing up his haka. "Look, bro, I know you're ready to fight, and I don't doubt your courage one bit. But if you see me start to—change—then it really will be time for you to run for your life. I won't know what I'm doing at that point. Just trust me—if I change, you *run*, and don't look back."

He gave me that Dwayne Johnson eyebrow waggle again and smiled. "If you say so, I guess. But I gotta get me a piece of whatever's coming through the gate, yeah? So maybe you just hang back and toss that spear, and let Hemi's war club win some *mana* for us both."

Before I could respond, the gates burst open in an explosion of blue sparks and light, and then the Dullahan charged right for us.

EIGHTEEN

Journal Entry—9 Months, 16 Days A.J.

Peyote. I can't believe this... I'm road-tripping to South Texas with Belladonna to find an illegal plant with psychedelic properties. Nope, couldn't be something completely legal, like holding a séance or using a crystal ball. Finn's plan just had to involve collecting an illegal controlled substance. Great.

Apparently there are only a few places in the state where this stuff still grows, because between the drug dealers, hippies, and shaman types, they've practically harvested the plant out of existence. Supposedly if you're a member of the Native American Church you can collect this stuff legally. But since I'm not even one-sixty-fourth Native American, I have to go all Breaking Bad.

Damn it. I'm too pretty to go to prison.

-McC

. . .

AUSTIN, Texas—Present Day

As soon as the Dullahan entered the yard, the runes on the dock roof's support posts flared up with a brilliant gold light. The light arced out from each, connecting with the fence line and the secondary wards I'd set under the gate, arcing one final time to conclude the light show with a deep, reverberating *whoomp*. With the completion of the spell the Dullahan's magical connection to Underhill would be severed, and while that wouldn't stop him, it would severely reduce the limits of his stamina and strength. In short, my magical trap had just made this a fair fight.

The horse staggered as the spell cut off the Dullahan's power; whether because it was also linked to the Underrealms, or because it could sense its master's distress, I had no idea. Regardless, I could tell that the horseman keenly felt the loss of his magic, and watched as he swayed slightly in the saddle. He quickly recovered, raising his battle axe in his right hand and spurring his horse to charge at me.

I dove out of the way, but it wasn't necessary. Hemi ran at the Dullahan's horse like a defensive end on a quarterback blitz. The big man collided with the horse, shoulder first, and drove the great beast's trajectory off such that it would have missed me by a mile. Both horse and rider recovered, pivoting with precision as the horseman swung that huge axe of his like a scythe chopping wheat. With each swing, Hemi leaned back just out of reach, his eyes searching for an opening. Finally, he dove under a swing, striking the Dullahan's leg with the edge of his flat club and putting a deep dent in the horseman's silver greaves.

By that time, I had snuck around behind our enemy. I took that opportunity to throw my spear at his back. But somehow he sensed the attack and spun his axe behind him, deflecting my spear and sending it flying away to pierce the door of a Volkswagen some thirty feet distant. As it struck I reached out to the spear and made a pulling gesture in the air; with the sound of metal scraping metal, the spear freed itself from the door panel and flew back into my hand.

The Dullahan had recovered quickly and was advancing on Hemi. The Maori warrior was impressive, but there was only so much he could do with that short club of his against the reach and mass of the Dullahan's axe. He continued to dance back and lightly deflect the axe's blade with his club, never giving more ground than was necessary to avoid certain death.

Unfortunately, I saw what Hemi could not: the Dullahan was herding him into a dead end formed by two stacks of stripped car frames and the junkyard fence. Soon Hemi would have no place to go, and he'd be trapped and at the mercy of the horseman's axe.

"Screw it," I said to myself as I threw the spear again, this time not at the horseman but at his steed. I aimed for one of its fetlocks and the spear pierced it cleanly, causing the animal to falter. For a moment I felt horrible about harming it, then reminded myself that it was likely another fae—perhaps an *aughiskey*, a *púca* or a *nuckalevee*—who served the Dullahan in exchange for the opportunity to eat his victims. If so, it would heal soon after leaving the junkyard, once its connection to Underhill was restored.

I called the spear back to my hand, just as the Dullahan reared back for another swing at Hemi. The big man just stood there, waiting to be struck down. *Move!* But he couldn't; he'd reached the end of the line and had nowhere else to go. The Maori crossed his arms in front of him and the glow from his tattoos intensified —a sign that he was bracing for impact.

I doubted it would be enough. Desperate, I threw the spear as hard as I could, not at the Dullahan, but at his axe. The spear tip caught the beveled edge of the axe's blade, torquing it in the horseman's hand just enough so the flat of the axe struck and not the edge. A tremendous noise, like a clap of thunder, rose from the impact. Hemi was lifted up into the air and collided with the corrugated metal fence, flying through it and into the street.

"Hemi!" I shouted. I spotted him through the hole in the fence, lying unconscious halfway on the curb across the road. Angered by the sight, I called my spear back to me and readied myself to charge the Dullahan, just as he cantered his horse and nudged it around to face me.

Suddenly Finn came running out from the depths of the junkyard, screaming and waving a gnarled old staff overhead like Gandalf on the walls of Minas Tirith. He was only half-clothed, and unfortunately it was the top half and not the bottom. His white hair and beard flew everywhere, and speckles of froth shot from his mouth as he roared. I assumed he'd just woken up from one of his drunken, drug-fueled stupors, and had decided to come out and commit suicide by headless horseman. *Wonderful.*

He screamed with rage as he advanced on the Dullahan. "You fae think I'm just a washed-up old man, but I still have a few tricks up my sleeve. Long has it been since the Tuatha dared the wrath of Finnegas the Seer, and it's high time I reminded you why that is!"

With all the racket Finn was making, the Dullahan turned toward him. The pale gray head under his arm laughed silently at what it saw. Based on Finn's reaction, I didn't think that was the best idea. Okay, so the old man's naughty bits were flopping around all over the place and he was foaming at the mouth, but I was fairly certain he wasn't kidding about having a few cards left to play. Sure enough, Finn chanted in a dialect of ancient Gaelic that few of the fae even remembered, and then he threw a handful of colored pebbles into the air.

The stones landed in a circle around the Dullahan, and for a few seconds nothing happened. I wondered if it were true, that the old man had finally been spent and used up like last week's lunch money. Under its arm the horseman's face seemed to laugh even harder, and although his head never made a sound, his body shook with mirth. It was one of the creepier things I'd ever seen, and it sent a chill up my spine in spite of the anger and shame I felt for my mentor.

Then the ground around the Dullahan began to shake, and the wounded horse stumbled and fell to one knee. The horseman attempted to urge it back up, perhaps to make his escape, but it was too late. The earth beneath them opened up in a huge gaping maw, swallowing horse and rider both in a single gulp. I observed as they tumbled into sheer blackness below, my own mouth agape as I watched the hole close up as if it had never been there at all.

I turned in amazement to Finn, who was now leaning against a rusted old Cadillac that was missing its doors, windshield, and hood. There was an ozone scent in the air left over from my wards and the spell Finn had just cast. Besides the sound of the old man gasping to catch his breath, the junkyard was eerily still.

"Where did you send him?" I asked.

The old man sagged and held up a finger, panting like a dog. "Sent him—far away—to the Underrealms. He won't—be back—anytime soon, I think."

I nodded, hesitant to show him the least bit of gratitude. Then I remembered Hemi and ran through the hole in the fence to see if he was even alive. As I ducked through the fence, a red Porsche peeled away from the curb across the street in a cloud of tire smoke. *Second time I've seen that car*, I reflected. Unfortunately, the angle was no good and I couldn't get a read on the plates before they turned the corner. *Damn it.*

Frustrated, I ran across the street to check on Hemi. He was breathing and had a pulse, but was still out cold. I hefted him over my shoulders in a fireman's carry and hauled him back inside the junkyard. Laying him down on the dock, I snatched a discarded piece of seat foam from nearby to use as a pillow for his huge head. Finn stumbled over and began checking him out, nodding with relief after a brief examination.

"He'll be fine. His wards saved him. Whoever tattooed these designs on him knew what they were doing. I haven't seen work this good since the third century BC."

"So no permanent damage, then?"

He shook his head. "None that I can see. But he's going to have one hell of a headache when he comes back around."

I sighed with relief. "The red caps have Sabine, Finn. I need you to tell me how to find them."

"Those money-grubbing little bastards, I knew they wouldn't leave it alone." He hocked and spat, hitting a hubcap a few feet away. "Rocko's been trying to get me to do more work for him, but I keep refusing. It's why they were beating me up the other night."

I growled in response. "Just what kind of work are we talking about here, Finn?"

He squirmed, and not because he was naked from the waist down. "I was enchanting their drugs to make them more addictive."

I took a deep breath, preparing to tear into him, but he held a hand up and surprised me by admitting to being an asshole.

"I know, it's a damned shitty thing to do. But they were giving me oxy and heroin for free, so long as I kept using alchemical magic to enchant their dope. It was only when I decided to clean up and get off the stuff that I realized how low I'd really gotten. I refused to do it for them anymore, and they didn't take it very well."

I nodded. "Why didn't you put the whammy on them like you did to the Dullahan a few minutes ago?"

He shrugged. "Withdrawal and the lingering effects

of long-term opiate addiction. I'm still not myself, and may not be for some time yet. I'm actually surprised I was able to pull that spell off, but I guess I was pretty damned angry." He paused and rubbed his ear. "Angry at myself, too."

"Yeah, join the club. I'd like to sit here and catch up with the clean and sober version of you, but I need to find the Syndicate and you need to go put some pants on. Can you please tell me where I can find those punks?"

His face soured and he made a show of scratching his sack. Yep, that was my mentor: the greatest druid ever, proving once again he'd become an uncouth jack-ass. I was seriously glad no one was around to witness this sad scene.

"They work out of Rocko's bar, a place called The Bloody Fedora down on Industrial off South First, behind the all-nude titty bar. Cinder block, bars on the windows, painted a sickly green color—you can't miss it."

"Bloody Fedora. Subtle. Anything I should know before I head down there?"

"Take some back up. I'm fairly certain they have a troll working security and an ogre tending bar. Hard to say for sure, though—I was messed up pretty bad every time I went down there. But expect trouble."

"Great. Thanks for the warning."

He looked down at Hemi. "Sure you don't want to wait for your friend to wake up?"

"Nah, I don't want to drag him any further into this if I don't have to. Besides, the longer I wait, the greater the chance they'll start carving pieces off Sabine. I'll call Belladonna; she owes me a favor anyway."

"Ah, the harlot on the Harley. I like her, you should bring her around more often." He made a crude thrusting motion with his hips.

I closed my eyes, turned away, and extended both my hands to hide his nether regions from view. "Oh, for Pete's sake, this is not a conversation I want to have with you in your current state of undress. Now, I'm off to rescue Sabine."

Disgusted beyond even my high tolerance for crude humor, I pivoted and made a beeline for my scooter while shouting over my shoulder to make certain I was heard.

"And for the love of all that's holy, put some pants on before Hemi wakes up, or you can bet that the Dullahan and those garden gnomes are going to be the least of your problems."

NINETEEN

Journal Entry—9 Months, 19 Days A.J.

Well, this just keeps getting better and better. Seems that Bells and I have provoked the ire of the local peyotero, who also happens to be a skinwalker. I hate skinwalkers. They're always bad news, and way worse than 'thropes.

The reason I hate skinwalkers so much is because they're like ninja werewolves that also use magic. There ain't nuthin simple about fighting a damned skinwalker.

Right now we're camped out in the middle of nowhere, close to Rio Grande City. We snuck on some ranch to go peyote hunting, because everything down here is private property, and apparently we walked smack in the middle of this skinwalker's peyote-hunting territory.

I have to go, because it's my turn to take watch. If we

manage to get back home safely, I'm going to strangle Finn.

-McC

AUSTIN, Texas—Present Day

Bells met me behind The Bloody Fedora about a half-hour after I called her. Being the professional she was, she'd parked her Harley at the strip club and jumped the fence that separated the two properties. She was wearing a long, black leather trench coat that somehow still showed off her athletic figure. It was split up the back to allow for easy movement, and I suspected she had numerous knives and other weapons hidden within. The hilt of a short sword poked up over her shoulder, and a brief flash of chrome from inside her coat told me she was packing.

I'd taken the time to change into my "urban" hunting gear while I waited. I kept all that stuff inside my Crane-skin Bag, and had hidden behind a dumpster while getting it all on. Back in my days with Jesse, we preferred wearing motorcycle leathers, gloves, and boots. Since then my enchanting abilities had improved considerably, so I'd graduated to clothing that stood out less and allowed better freedom of movement.

I'd learned over the years that doing night ops in the city often meant entering dance clubs, bars, and the odd formal gathering. So I'd learned to dress less like a ninja biker, and more like a club hopper... or club security. I was wearing a pair of polished black leather jump boots, dark gray cargo pants that were tailored to pass for a pair of casual dress slacks, a white dress shirt, and my dad's military rain coat—a long black trench that was both rugged and loose enough to move in.

Had I been hunting in the countryside, I'd be wearing less formal attire. Still, everything I wore had been spelled and warded to provide protection of some sort. The boots were enchanted to give me traction, even on slick surfaces. The pants and coat had been warded such that they'd deflect most blades and even small arms fire. And the shirt was stitched with runes to protect me against glamours and mind control spells.

I had my Craneskin Bag strapped over my shoulder, but hidden inside my coat. It always looked more or less empty and laid flat against my side, so no one would even know it was there. Inside the bag I had all my surprises ready to go, and also had a few weapons hidden on my person in case I couldn't reach my bag. I was pissed, and had dressed for action. I just hoped things wouldn't get out of hand so I wouldn't lose control.

Belladonna strutted up, her heels clicking on the asphalt as she walked over to where I leaned against the back wall of the bar.

"Hey handsome, don't you look smashing this evening," she cooed.

"Thanks for coming, Bells. And, um, you look nice too."

She smirked and narrowed her eyes slightly. "Weak, but it'll do."

I pursed my lips in frustration. "Sorry, I'm just not good at this sort of thing, like paying compliments or reading people's emotions. Jesse and I just sort of understood each other—"

"—and since you haven't dated in oh, forever, you've never really picked up those skills." She walked up to me and stood on her tiptoes, kissing me lightly on the cheek. "Colin, I know you much better than you think. At heart, you're a sweet guy who bumbles through life and relationships, because you're in love with a ghost. But I'm a hunter—I know how to wait."

I stood there, speechless, and she pivoted toward the club, gesturing grandly with one arm. "So this is the castle we're storming. I hope the girl's worth it."

I found my voice again, and licked my lips to ensure I wouldn't mumble. "I know you don't care for Sabine much, so thanks for doing this."

She waved my thanks off and shrugged. "She's not so bad, sugar—but just not the one for you. And besides, since Crowley got his codpiece all in a bundle, you're the only partner I can count on to back me up."

I snuck over to a window and examined the bars outside. "Speaking of which, as much as I hate the guy I wouldn't mind having him around this evening. Whatever happened between you two, anyway? If you don't mind me asking."

"Oh, I don't mind. We dated, we slept together, and I decided I couldn't stand his creep. He's cute enough, I suppose, but it was his magic that clinched it for me. Smelled like cat piss and rotten flowers, and it hung on him all the time."

She leaned in close to me and took a long whiff. "Not like you, loverboy—you smell like pinecones, musk, and freshly-turned dirt. Yum."

"Um, thanks?"

She huffed and crossed her arms. "You're supposed to compliment me now, silly. Duh. How'd you ever even get to first base with Jesse? You seriously have zero game."

"Well, I—I like the way you fight?" It came out as a question, more than a statement, but it was true. Belladonna could throw down, and I liked that about her.

"Hmmm..." she hummed as she rubbed her chin. "Okay, I feel you. Kind of nice to have someone appreciate me for all the hard work I put in at the gym."

I sighed in relief.

"But you didn't even notice the new perfume I'm wearing."

Trying hard not to groan, I shifted my sight into the magical spectrum and began working on the alarm spell on the window. "Let's talk about this over drinks after we rescue Sabine, alright?"

"Colin, did you just ask me on a date?"

"You're incorrigible, Bells. Seriously incorrigible."

She flipped her hair with pride. "I know—it's why you keep me around."

I chuckled. "You're a good friend, Bells. And I don't have many friends."

"Hush now, I'm not going anywhere. Now, get that freaking window open so we can jump these clowns and kick some ass. I've made zero progress on the fae killings, I haven't been laid in weeks, and to be honest, I need a little stress relief."

I nodded once. "Alrighty then, your wish is my command," I bypassed the alarm spell and magically popped the lock on the window bars.

"Careful there, stud—you might commit to something you aren't prepared to handle."

Belladonna grabbed the iron security bars as they swung out, using them to vault herself up on the window ledge. She peered inside before jimmying the lock on the window with a slender, deadly-looking knife, and then pulled the window open.

"Coast is clear. Looks like an office in here." She looked back at me and gave a wicked grin as she balanced, catlike, on the sill. "Do try to keep up," she quipped, slipping out of sight.

———

ONCE INSIDE, I cracked the door and threw a small chrysoberyl sphere out into the hall. The cat's eye rolled to the wall and hugged the baseboard, continuing to wind its way out to the bar. I waited until it had made a circumference of the place and rolled back inside the office where we hid, stopping at the tip of my boot.

I picked the stone up, closed my eyes, and rolled it around between my palms, concentrating to read the sound energy it had recorded as it traversed the area. Within moments a sort of sonar map formed in my head, giving me information on the layout of the place, where the patrons and staff were located, and how much resistance we might encounter if we had to fight our way out.

I opened my eyes. "C'mon, no one's in the hall. Let's go check the other rooms to make sure they don't have Sabine here."

"I could've told you that two minutes ago, druid-boy."

Belladonna pointed at a TV monitor on the wall with a smirk. The screen was split into four sections, and each displayed feeds from CCTV cameras stationed in various areas of the bar.

"Fine, next time I'll let you be in charge of scouting and intelligence." I pocketed the stone in the interior of my coat and stepped out into the hall. The sounds of bottles clinking and billiard balls colliding echoed from the other end. Out here, the place smelled of cigarettes, sour beer, and desperation.

I turned quickly and ducked down the hall with Belladonna on my heels. We checked the bathrooms, finding them empty, then came to a door labeled "Employees Only!" It sounded like someone was being tortured inside. I could definitely hear a woman groaning as if she were in pain, as well as someone grunting with exertion. I tried the knob; it was locked. A quick cantrip popped the latch, and I burst into the room.

The open door revealed a very out of breath Sal, pumping his little buttocks away behind a human woman on her knees, her red pleather miniskirt hiked up around her waist and a pair of neon green thong underwear pulled down to her thighs. They were both in the throes of... something, but I hesitated to call it passion.

Regardless, it took a moment for the pair to notice they had company. Before they could react, I snapped a picture with my phone. Bells already had a gun on them, and closed the door behind us. I crossed my arms and leaned against the doorframe, turning toward her with a smirk.

"Some things just cannot be unseen." I pointed at the lady. "Miss, cover yourself please. And you—" I gestured at Sal, who was desperately trying to get his pants pulled up. "What would Mrs. Sal and all your mini-Sals think?"

"Wait just a minute, druid, this ain't what you think—"

Belladonna laughed humorlessly. "Oh, it's exactly what we think. When we walked in, you were laying twenty feet of pipe down on Miss Thing here, three inches at a time. Yeah, you just got caught red-handed, red cap."

I turned and fist-bumped her. "Nice one." She lifted her chin at me smugly.

I started thumbing through my phone. "Let's see if we can find Mrs. Sal's profile on Faebook. Ah, here she is. Aw, Sal Jr. looks just like you." I held the phone up to show Belladonna, who wiggled her hand in front of her.

"Meh, looks like he takes after her side of the family." I leaned in and we shared the screen, closely examining the photo.

"You're right. Still has his eyes though."

The woman on the floor turned around and smacked Sal. "You told me you were single, asshole!"

Sal covered up and flinched away. "Cinnamon, I can explain!"

Belladonna leaned over to me and mouthed a single word behind her hand. *Stripper.*

I chose not to pass judgment, since I had more pressing matters to attend. "Sal, bottom line is that with a few keystrokes I can easily ruin your marriage and put you in child support hell. Do you really want that, or can we come to some other arrangement?"

His shoulders sagged, and he held up his hands, deflated. "Alright, alright! The girl's not here. Rocko sent Johnny Dibs and Tony G to take her out to some farm-house outside of town, about two hours ago."

I cocked my head and stared at Sal sideways. "Wait a minute—what farmhouse?"

He rubbed his hands together nervously. "You know, the one where that creepy wizard lives, same place they iced those elves and 'thropes before they dumped 'em." He pointed at Belladonna. "She knows where it is. Heck, she was banging the guy for a while."

I turned to Bells. "Is he talking about Crowley?"

Belladonna gave Sal a viper's glare and pointed one perfectly manicured finger at him. She lowered the barrel of the pistol in her hand about fifteen degrees.

"You watch your mouth, shorty, or you're going to get spontaneous sexual reassignment surgery." She glanced at me out of the corner of her eye. "Yeah, I think so. He has a place out near McKinney Roughs, along the Colorado River. Turned a grain silo into his wizard's tower or something. The silo thing is tacky as hell, but the kitchen's kind of cute."

I snapped my fingers and pulled out Elias' phone. "Son of a bitch—I guess now we know who's behind all those killings." I pulled up the GPS app and tossed the phone to her. "Take a look at this."

She glanced down at the phone screen. "Yep, that's his place alright. Where'd you get this?"

I looked over at Sal, deciding that I didn't want to tip my hand. "Tell you later. Sal, buddy, I have you by the balls. We're going to slip out of here, and I swear if you warn anyone we're coming—"

He waved both hands in the air. "Hey, you got nothin' to worry about from me. My old lady finds out about this, and she'll be wearing my nuts for earrings. You go do your thing, and I'll keep Cinnamon here under wraps till we close up."

Cinnamon began to protest, but Sal pulled out a roll of bills and tossed two hundreds at her. "And two more at the end of the night, for keeping your mouth shut."

Belladonna holstered her pistol and wagged a finger at Cinnamon. "I say take the money, sugar—this asshole's not good to you for much else."

Cinnamon stood up and tucked the bills in her blouse, avoiding making eye contact while she straightened herself up. Then she proceeded to slap the living crap out of Sal, who for the most part took it like a man. I felt sorry for her, but helping a young girl with self-esteem issues wasn't very high on my list at the moment. We both watched in awe until she finished.

Bells whistled. "Damn, I bet that felt *good*."

I pushed off the wall to go and addressed the now bloodied dwarf.

"One last thing, Sal—I'm going to need the keys to your car." He rubbed his face, smearing blood and snot everywhere, then gave a small shake of his head before tossing me a set of keys with a rabbit's foot keychain attached.

I took a small bow before exiting the room. "Thank you, both, for your cooperation." Sal just waved me off and sulked, and Cinnamon flipped us off as we left.

Belladonna turned to me as we slipped out of the storage room. "Too bad. I was just beginning to like that girl."

TWENTY

Journal Entry—9 Months, 20 Days A.J.

Belladonna and I stayed up all night, keeping an eye out for the skinwalker. We kept seeing ghost lights all over the place, and Belladonna said they were probably spirits that the skinwalker trapped, spying on us for him.

That made me wonder if he could trap Jesse's spirit. I really don't want to think about it. Besides, I never really seem to feel her presence anywhere but at my mom's house. I guess it's because that's where we—you know, first time and all that. The books Belladonna "borrowed" from the Circle's library mention that spirits often need a strong emotional anchor to remain in this world.

Kind of makes me sad to think about it, because she's all alone right now. Hopefully we can wrap things up here and get back home, before this skinwalker sneaks up on us Blair Witch style and skins us both.

-McC

AUSTIN, Texas—Present Day

Crowley's place turned out to be an old farmhouse overlooking the Colorado River, right next door to Barton Hills Farm. It was too early for the place to be open to the public yet, which was a bit of a relief. If a fight erupted—and chances of that were nearly one-hundred percent at this point—then I didn't want anybody getting curious and wandering onto Crowley's land. When I pulled up to the front gate, I saw his name on the mailbox—and he had a big gold "C" welded on the wrought iron gate. *Chalk one up for ostentation.*

The gate was locked, and I didn't want to risk setting off an alarm. So, I parked Sal's painstakingly restored 1972 Olds 88 (the perfect pimpmobile for the discerning minuscule mobster), and got out to wait for Belladonna. She had refused to ride with me, saying that she needed time to process the whole Crowley being involved with kidnapping and killing thing. I for one was glad that I'd borrowed Sal's ride, since it was warm inside and way more practical for such a long drive. He'd had blocks on the pedals and a booster in the seat, but once I'd gotten rid of them it was good to go. Even though it drove like a boat, it was a hell of a lot faster than my scooter.

Bells pulled up and jumped off her bike shortly after

I'd parked, shaking her hair out as she removed her helmet. Based on her body language, I could tell she was pissed and that she'd worked herself into a frenzy on the way over. She slammed her helmet down on her seat, then reached into her saddle bags and pulled out a short-barreled 12-gauge pump shotgun, racking a round in the chamber as she walked over. She gestured at the gate with the barrel of the gun.

"Is it locked? Good." I jumped back when I realized what she had in mind, just as she blasted the padlock on the gate with a few rounds of double-ought buckshot. The brass casing on the lock shattered, and she was just about to rip it off and push the gate open when I reached out to stop her. Not that I was worried about the gunshots; shotgun blasts were a common enough occurrence in the Texas countryside. However, I was concerned she'd trigger an alarm by opening the gate.

"Hang on, hang on—I get that you're pissed, but we're dealing with a mage here. Gimme a second to see what sort of wards and alarms he has."

A quick inspection showed there were only a few wards and one alarm spell. I fiddled with the alarm, taking a few minutes to disable it without making our presence known. Luckily, the other wards were merely there for protection from fae, vamps, weres, curses, and such, and wouldn't keep us from entering the premises. Apparently, Crowley thought he would be nigh on invincible in his own demesne. Naturally, I intended to disabuse him of that notion.

After dealing with the alarm spell, I took a few extra moments to study the other wards carefully. Upon closer inspection, I realized one of those wards was designed to keep something *in*, instead of keeping things out. I made note of it, since it could come in handy later, and spent a few moments studying it just to be sure I understood the weaves and patterns Crowley had used to cast it. Admittedly it was good work, and he was a far more powerful magic-user than I was. But I was smarter and much better-looking, and I could easily alter that spell to get the effect I desired.

Once finished with my inspection and magical B&E work, I motioned for Bells to follow me. "Don't open the gate—it'll trigger the alarm spell I just bypassed. Just hop it for now, and we can blow it up on the way out if you like."

Belladonna growled. "Promises, promises."

I jumped the fence, then gave her an unnecessary hand down as she followed me over. The fact that she took it meant she was mad enough to kick some ass, but not angry enough to completely lose her shit. That was totally cool, because my plan didn't actually involve her fighting Crowley at all, and I didn't need her going off half-cocked before we rescued Sabine.

Once we'd cleared the gate, we headed toward the

house. But we'd gone no more than twenty or thirty feet when I stumbled in a deep depression in the dirt and gravel driveway.

"Bells, look at this." I pointed at the hole I'd tripped over, which was in the shape of a lone, massive footprint, roughly two-and-a-half feet long and four inches deep.

She looked at the footprint and whistled. "Holy shit, I can't believe it. He has a freaking *fachen*."

We shared a knowing, tense look. Fachen were perhaps the most fearsome creatures mentioned in ancient Irish mythology, said to be the direct descendants of the Fomorians. They were giants, but malformed and hideous in the very worst way. Fachen only had one leg, one arm, and half a torso. You'd think they'd be practically helpless, but legend had it that they were fast, brutally strong, and that their one arm could magically swivel to either side of their body.

Fachen were also said to prefer flexible weapons like flails or long spiked chains. They were living, breathing wrecking machines; a lone fachen was rumored to have destroyed an entire forest with a massive chain in a single night. How Crowley had bound one into service was anyone's guess, but it was definitely not something that two mortals like myself and Belladonna could take on alone, hunter and druid training or no.

I looked around nervously, but the fact was if this massive creature was still around, we'd hear it before we saw it. As we approached the farmhouse and outbuild-ings, we switched to using hand signals instead of verbal communication. Fact was, we really had no idea who or what might be out here guarding Crowley's place, in addition to the fachen. I figured if we were careful we might have a small chance of maintaining stealth and getting Sabine out clean.

The farmhouse was empty and devoid of any signs of habitation. According to Belladonna, Crowley lived in a converted silo that sat adjacent to one of the barns. Why someone would buy a house and not live in it was beyond me, but then again I didn't understand much about how wealthy people spent their money. Bells had mentioned a few times that Crowley was loaded, and in my experience, trust fund babies were ridiculously clue-less about the actual value of things. Someone who needed a home could have been living in that house, but instead it sat empty. Hell, I could have been living in that house, instead of a junkyard. All I could do was give a mental head shake and move on.

When we reached the first barn, Bells signaled that she sensed activity inside. I threw my magic marble out, and it rolled around the corner and under the barn door. It showed me there were two very tall and thin bipeds inside, and revealed an unconscious third figure in one of the horse stalls. I gave Belladonna the signal for trolls, and she nodded and drew her sword. I pulled a couple of tricks from my bag, preparing them for when we got the drop on these jokers.

Trolls were a particularly nasty species of unseelie fae. Originating in northern Europe, they had migrated and settled wherever people of Scandinavian descent roamed, which meant damned near everywhere. Unsavory types in the supernatural community liked to use them for muscle, because they were tough, dumb as rocks, and would work for pocket change. Literally, you could pay them in pocket change. So long as it was silver, they'd take it. Like I said, trolls were stupid.

But the bad thing about trolls was they were really tough. Most had limited powers of regeneration, and while they could be hurt, you could drop them and they'd get right back up to come at you again. They really only had two weaknesses: sunlight and fire. Sunlight would turn them to stone, so trolls tended to live in caves, swamps, and under bridges for the most part. But short of shooting them in the head and dragging them into sunlight (which meant you had to dispose of a very heavy body at that point), the only way to permanently kill them was to burn them.

I signaled Bells that we'd enter the barn on the count of three. I got to a one count before she mouthed something that could've been "bucket," and kicked the doors in—a pretty impressive feat, considering she was about five feet nothing. I sighed and followed her in, waiting for her to dismantle the trolls by sword and superior fire-power, at which point I would step in and finish the job.

They were each about seven feet tall, bipedal, and roughly humanoid in appearance. But that's where any similarities to humanity ended. Their skin was a mottled brownish-green color, and they were weirdly muscular, but in a way that was completely wrong to the human eye. The only way I could describe it was that they were *lumpy*. They had dull, black eyes that lacked pupils, sharp claws on their long alien hands, and tufts of hair growing in odd places all over their nearly naked bodies. Each wore scraps of human clothing that had to have been size 4XL or better, and their clothes hung off them in tatters. They were arguing over the remains of a cow's leg when we came in, and it looked like they were about to come to blows.

Trolls were frightening to behold, that was a fact, but the most fearsome thing about them was their smell. Imagine the worst foot odor possible combined with Limburger cheese, feces, and bad breath. Then, double it. That was what trolls smelled like. Routinely, people who hired them would also hire a mage to contain their smell, because if they didn't they'd have to torch anything the trolls touched once they were gone.

Unfortunately, Crowley had cast no such spell on these trolls, and as soon as Belladonna and I entered the room we both gagged and retched. That would explain why Sabine was unconscious, because an odor this bad had to have knocked her out. Instantly, my eyes watered as I fought the dry heaves.

The trolls each had a hand on the haunch of meat, and looked up at us as we stumbled in, coughing and hacking and trying not to puke. Despite the fact that my eyes were watering and I was coughing up a lung, I recognized one of them from Maeve's; it was the very same troll that had been guarding her front entrance.

He pointed at us with a long, gnarly finger, laughing as we coughed and wheezed. "Bah ha! Humans can't take troll pew. Good for us, bad for you, cause now we eat you too!"

Did I mention that trolls were horrible and compulsive poets?

Maeve's doorkeeper let go of the cow leg and picked up a log laying nearby. It pointed it at us as it began advancing. "Now, we eat you, make you into poo!"

The other troll flipped around the leg it held so it could use it as a weapon. "I get the big guy, he juicier than skinny little small fry."

The first troll turned back to his partner. "I get big guy or make you cry!"

"You no call, you lose all. Snooze-lose, cuz you no choose!"

"No snooze-lose! You lose, I eat youse!"

Soon they were trading blows, beating each other

with the log and the cow's leg. It would have been humorous, if I hadn't been fighting dry heaves the whole time.

Finally, Bells recovered enough to aim her shotgun, firing four shots in rapid succession. All four shots struck their intended targets, hitting each troll once in the torso and once in the head.

She patted my arm clumsily as she staggered out of the barn. "Please, burn those things now, before they start talking again." Then she disappeared around the corner of the barn and began vomiting.

First, I covered my mouth with my shirt and went into the stall where I suspected Sabine had been placed. She was bound and gagged, and had small pieces of vomit around her mouth. Her glamour had faded, and despite her current sad state I noted that she was just as lovely and intact as ever. I picked her up and carried her outside the barn, gently laying her down and checking for a pulse; it was weak, but there.

Angered by what had been done to my friend, I entered the barn again and produced two baby food jars from my pockets. Each had a wax seal around the lid, and they contained an alchemical mixture of grain alcohol, turpentine, oil, phosphorous, and magnesium. Basically they were the magical version of white phosphorous grenades, and they'd ensure that the trolls stayed dead for good. I tossed each in turn at the bodies, chanting a short spell as I threw them that would cause the jars to detonate on impact. The trolls were already starting to stir, and as each bomb struck and spread liquid fire over their bodies, they shrieked and writhed on the dirt floor of the barn.

The smell of the burning trolls was even worse than their normal smell, if that were even possible, so I quickly retreated from the building. Outside, I found that Belladonna had recovered. She was in the process of removing Sabine's gag, untying her, and wiping her face off with a wet wipe. As I approached, she tossed me a travel pack of wipes.

"Just in case you hurled and need to clean up—I never do a job without them. Honestly, what kind of slob lets trolls on their property without casting an odor removal spell on them? It blows my mind that he could put up with that. Ugh."

I pulled a wipe out of the package and held it under my nose, taking a deep whiff of the soap and baby powder scent it contained. "Well, one thing's for sure: he wasn't planning on keeping this place. Once those trolls stunk up that barn, it became completely unusable and unsellable—and for a barn, that's saying something. That means he must be planning to leave here once he finishes whatever he's been doing."

On cue, a bright light flared from an upper-story

window in the nearby converted silo. Bells pointed in the general direction of the silo and shook her head.

"That's his laboratory. Looks like he's working some serious magic up there—not good." She stood and beckoned me. "Come on, we need to find out what he's up to and stop him."

I looked down at Sabine and back to Belladonna. "First, we need to get her someplace safe. No telling what else is roaming around on this farm. We leave her here and she's as good as dead."

Belladonna scowled and nodded. "You're right. But as soon as she's safe, I'm coming back here to kick that bastard's ass." She punched her fist into her palm and glared at the silo.

"There'll be enough time for that later," I lied. "Just watch my back while I get her to the car, and then you can do all the ass-kicking you want." I carefully picked Sabine up in my arms and headed toward the front gate.

TWENTY-ONE

Journal Entry—9 Months, 22 Days A.J.

Well, nothing surprises me anymore. We were out roaming around in the brush, trying to find some peyote, when we came across this older woman who was harvesting medicinal plants. Turns out she's a curandera, which is sort of like a local wise woman. She asked what the hell two gringos were doing out in the middle of the desert in South Texas, so we told her our story.

Leticia—that's her name—said she knew the peyotero we'd pissed off, and that she'd try to talk him into letting us have some of his stuff. Whatever. I have rocks in my shoes, dust in every crack and crevice, and I've been stung and stuck so many times I can't count how many cactus needles I've pulled out of my body. South Texas is way less hospitable than the Hill Country. Note to self: never buy land near the border.

I know, I know... some druid I turned out to be; I can't even find a simple plant without help. Belladonna says I'm just off my game right now. Hopefully Leticia will have some luck with convincing this skinwalker to help us, because right now I just want to take a shower and a nap.

-McC

AUSTIN, Texas—Present Day

A few minutes later we stood by the gate, and I nodded at the fence. "Bells, you'll have to climb over first so I can hand her to you."

Belladonna complied and vaulted the fence. I climbed a short way up the gate then handed Sabine over to her, and she carried Sabine to the back seat of Sal's car. As soon as she turned her back to me I went to work altering the weaves on the containment spell, changing the spell parameters so it would keep every living creature present trapped on the property—and keep everything else out until dawn.

I slapped my hands down on the gate, chanting and releasing my magic to activate the barrier, and locking it with a deadman's timer that would prevent anyone from canceling the spell before dawn. If anyone tampered with that ward before sunrise it'd shock them into next week, kind of like the world's deadliest electric fence. A pale blue light flared up all along the fence line, dimming after a few seconds to shimmer softly in the dark.

When Belladonna saw what I had done, she sprinted toward the gate, only to be repelled by the wards as she approached.

"Colin, you dick!" she cried. "Let me in this second, or so help me I'm going to kick your ass after Crowley is through with you!"

I shook my head slowly. "Sorry, Bells, but I can't let you help with this. For one, you can't defeat Crowley—he's just too strong. And if that fachen shows up, you know there's only one way anybody is leaving this place alive."

She reached out to me, pulling up just short of the magical barrier. "Colin, you can't. Once the Circle finds out you've had another episode, they'll hunt you mercilessly. You'll never be able to live in peace."

"I have to, Bells. I already lost Jesse, and there's no way I'm going to lose you too." I looked at the silo in the distance. "If I don't come out at dawn, notify the Circle and bring them back here to raze this place to the ground."

Bells just bit her lip and nodded. Without another word, I turned and ran for the silo, trying not to think about the fact that it was the first time I'd ever seen her cry.

I KNEW that the fachen was around somewhere, and I also knew it would likely be hiding behind a see-me-not charm or some sort of shadow spell. And since Crowley was simply that much better than me at magic, the chances that I would see it coming were nil to none. My only saving grace was the fact that it was damned hard to hide environmental effects of movement with magic. Even a complete invisibility spell (very hard to do, by the way) couldn't cover for you if you knocked something off a table or rustled a curtain. Those were the sort of things that typically gave someone away, no matter how good their see-me-not or invisibility spell might be.

Considering how big this fachen was, it was a good bet that I'd be able to sense its approach. Something that big would cause the ground to shake every time it moved, and it would break branches and trample foliage with every hopping step. As long as I was paying attention to my environment, I *should* have the ability to avoid an ambush.

Still, I tried to maintain as much stealth as possible as I advanced on the silo. I triggered my own see-me-not cantrip—a weak but usually adequate spell I had woven into my dad's overcoat—clinging to the shadows made by buildings and trees as I made my way to the silo. Crowley was clearly working on something big in there.

Every minute or so, bright lights flashed from the windows, and a sound like thunder drowned out the sounds made by the wind rustling through the trees and grass.

The barn where we'd left the trolls to burn was on fire now, and bound to draw the attention of the fachen and any other creatures who might have been guarding Crowley's silo. I decided to use that to my advantage, and snuck around the far side of the tower to approach it from the shadows cast by the flames. The moment I made it to the silo's walls, I felt a vibration through the ground beneath me.

Thrum... Thrum... THRUM. The fachen approached. I ducked down into the shadow of the silo wall and tried to use my second sight to determine where it was. At first, there was nothing to indicate its presence, but then I began to notice a large anomaly moving around the barn. It wasn't so much a distortion of energies, but rather a feeling of something that was *not there* at all. Crowley's shadow magic was strong and he was a highly skilled mage, much better than I had given him credit for; but once I knew what to look for, it was easy for me to determine the fachen's position.

And, it was huge—easily five meters tall or more. It hopped around in a manner reminiscent of a giant kangaroo or jack rabbit, and from what I could tell it was much faster and more graceful than one might expect from such a large creature. The fachen circled the barn several times, sniffing loudly and grumbling as it wandered the area, and then it began to search the other outbuildings. I took that as a sign that I'd better duck inside the silo before it found me out.

The entry to the silo was straight out of a high fantasy novel, which stood in stark contrast to the corrugated, galvanized steel panels of the silo itself. The door was a massive oak thing, bound in iron and studded with huge hand-forged nails. Both wood and iron were etched with runes of protection and warding. I silently cursed as I read the runes, preparing to either do some quick magical lock-picking or find another way in. That's when I realized that the wards and spells on the door had been disabled.

Curious. I gently nudged the door to find that it was unlocked, and left slightly ajar. *Shit.*

Everything about this scenario screamed "trap," but I was too invested in seeing this whole mess through to the end to stop now. Sure, I could have waited for the Circle to show up in the morning, because I was certain Belladonna had already called it in. Yet, for the next several hours I was stuck in here with a sixteen-foot tall man-eating giant and a powerful wizard—one who may or may not have been in possession of a magical object that could slay a god. Not to mention that the wizard hated my guts and wanted me dead. The chances of me making it through the night without being discovered were slim to none, especially in light of the fact that Crowley apparently was already well aware of my presence.

So much for the element of surprise, I thought. But as they say, sometimes the only way out is through. Abandoning stealth, I pushed the door fully open and entered Crowley's home. Inside, it was surprisingly chic and modern, like something you might have seen on one of those TV home makeover shows. The entire place was decorated in what some would call a "country modern" style, with lots of bead-board and wainscoting, light pastel accent walls done in earth tones, and sconces and light fixtures that had that late 1800s, almost steampunk industrial look. Not at all what I would have expected from a shadow wizard, but I had to say that I loved what he'd done with the place.

I stalked through the first floor, following the circular layout of the structure until I located the stairs.

"Oh, a wrought-iron bannister—nicely done," I mumbled to myself as I headed up to the second floor. "I seriously have to find out who he hired to decorate this place." Someday I planned to move out of the junkyard, hopefully after I completed my grad degree, and when that day came I definitely wouldn't mind living in a pad like this one. Damned shame he was probably going to abandon it.

As I neared the second floor, I got my mind back on task and reached into my Craneskin Bag for a few "save my ass" tricks. I tucked one into the pocket of my over-coat, and kept the other in the palm of my hand. If every-thing worked out the way I planned, I'd take Crowley out without a fight, and thereby avoid triggering my ríastrad. I peeked around the corner of the entry to the second floor; it was a massive open library, with shelves running from floor to ceiling all the way around.

"Oh, now I'm really jealous," I whispered to myself. Thankfully, this level was empty and showed no signs of life. However, the racket from Crowley's magic was growing louder, and coming from the floor above. I looked around and spotted a ladder staircase. Flashes of light shone through the cracks in and around a trap door sitting above the ladder, in time with the thunder claps coming from above.

I took a deep breath and began climbing up. Pausing at the top, I listened intently during lulls in the thun-dering racket. Above, Crowley chanted in old Tuatha, a language Finn sometimes used when casting his most powerful spells. How the wizard had learned to speak an ancient fae dialect was beyond me. I had been of the impression that no one but the oldest living creatures remembered that language. I decided I was pretty well screwed and pushed open the trap door, throwing caution to the wind as I climbed up into Crowley's aerie.

The place looked just as you might expect: an open room with wood slat floors, brick walls, and a huge thaumaturgic circle etched into the floor, the type used both for summonings and for containing the effects of particularly nasty spells. Work tables and stacks of shelves leaned against the exterior walls, containing all manner of alchemical and scientific equipment. I noted Bunsen burners and beakers, jars and glasses filled with various liquids and preserved body parts (both human and nonhuman), dry chemicals in sealed containers, scales and measures, and neat rows of reference books and grimoires—except for those left open in various random spots around the room.

Crowley of course stood in the middle of the circle, chanting intently, moving his hands around a smooth, levitating stone sphere about six inches in diameter. Strange eldritch energies popped and crackled between his hands and the object, which was most certainly Maeve's missing tathlum. He paid me no mind as my eyes darted around the place, but the trap door slammed shut behind me as an imp popped into view a few feet to my right.

The little creature sat cross-legged on the edge of a shelf, resting its chin on its closed fist. It was grayish-green in color, roughly two feet tall, bald and hairless—

with pointed ears and a forked tail that swished around as it examined me.

The imp looked me up and down and rolled its eyes. "So, you're the one the master has been going on and on about. What a letdown. The way he spoke of you, I was expecting someone much more impressive."

He—if it was a he, because I didn't care to look closely enough to determine its sex—picked his nose and flicked goo off his finger at the circle, causing a shimmering green barrier of light to appear as it zapped the snot into a puff of white smoke.

The imp cleared his throat and pointed with his chin at the shimmering magical barrier. "Not a good idea to try to enter that circle right now. Probably fry you like a pork chop. The master told me to let you know he'd be with you in a moment. Make yourself at home in the meantime." Then the imp picked up a copy of *People* magazine from the shelf next to it, flipped it open to an earmarked page, and proceeded to ignore me.

Crowley was currently occupied, there was no way I was getting through that barrier, and I had no other option except to go back outside and get eaten by the fachen. So, I pulled up a chair and waited. After about five minutes, I grew bored and began walking around the place, admiring the wizard's lab as well as the impressive collection of magical tomes and references in his collection. He had all the usual stuff: *The Testament and Keys of Solomon, The Pythagorean Mysteries, The Picatrix,* works by Faust and Marlowe, *Le Petit Albert,* and the *Sefer Raziel Ha-Malakh.* But he also had more esoteric works, including some written in the ancient language of the Tuatha Dé Danann. I also spotted *The Book of Azathoth,* a rather suspect translation of *Unaussprechliche Kulte,* and what might have been a copy of *De Vermis Mysteriis.* Apparently, Crowley dealt in some seriously dark shit.

I reached for the last book, but stopped when the imp coughed loudly. "I wouldn't do that if I were you. The last idiot who opened that thing and tried to read it grew tentacles from her fingers and went mad. Last we heard she was locked up at the state hospital after shouting 'Ph'nglui mglw'nafh Cthulhu R'lyeh wgah'nagl fhtagn!' over and over again until her throat hemorrhaged. Personally, I think he just keeps it around to be mean."

I slowly backed away from the tome and placed my hands in my pockets. The imp flipped a page in his gossip rag and went back to ignoring me. I wandered around a few more minutes, then got bored and sat back down. After twiddling my thumbs for a while, I pulled out my phone and played through several levels of *Cut the Rope* while Crowley finished his business.

After waiting a good twenty minutes, Crowley's chanting increased in volume and intensity, and the peals of thunder and flashes of light grew closer and closer together. I squinted to avoid being blinded, stuffing my fingers in my ears to muffle the sound. With a final crash and a flash of amber light, the Tathlum split in two, revealing a bright glowing gem within.

TWENTY-TWO

Journal Entry— 9 Months, 23 Days A.J.

Leticia came through. But now I owe a skinwalker a huge favor. The guy's name is Ernesto, and for a malefic soul-sucking sorcerer who comports with spiritual denizens of evil from the nether realms, he's actually not a bad sort of fellow.

But all pleasantries aside, you don't become a skinwalker by holding charity bake sales and collecting blankets for the local orphanage, so I don't even want to think about what he's going to ask of me someday. All I know is that one day he'll call this favor in, but it's totally worth it to help Jesse.

Belladonna has turned out to be one hell of a good friend. Hopefully Jesse won't be too pissed that we've been spending so much time together. Right now we're headed back to central Texas, and we called ahead to tell

*Maureen to sober Finn up before we get there so he can
tell me how to make this concoction that's supposed to
allow me to talk with ghosts.*

-McC

AUSTIN, Texas—Present Day

The barrier around the summoning circle fizzled
and dissipated, and Crowley's face beamed with self-
satisfied delight.

"Dude, please tell me this wasn't a ploy to get
Belladonna the gaudiest engagement ring ever," I said,
standing up and taking a good look at the jewel Crowley
snatched from the air. The two halves of the Tathlum
fell to the floor with a thud as soon as he grabbed the
gem, which appeared to be a baseball-sized ruby that
looked suspiciously like a twenty-sided die. He stared at
it intently as he spoke.

"Sorry to keep you waiting," the wizard replied. "I
told the fachen to keep you away for another half-hour at
least. Once I started the ritual, there was really nothing
you could do to interrupt me, but by arriving early you
kind of ruined my dramatic timing."

"Yeah, well—he got distracted when the barn caught
on fire, so I snuck past him while he wasn't looking." I
knocked on one of the walls and looked around. "By the
way, I admire what you've done with the place. Those

copper sconces downstairs are killer. Personally, I would have gone with the Colonial style, but the sort of steam-punk-slash-modern-farmhouse-slash-Saruman's   tower thing you got going on here is really working for me."

He frowned and glanced at me briefly, then returned to gazing at the jewel in his hand. "That's what I can't stand about you, McCool. Everything's a joke to you, isn't it? You're a walking, talking, magical weapon of mass destruction, and yet you gallivant all over the city as if you're not a constant threat to millions of people."

"Hey, let's just get one thing clear—I do *not* galli-vant. What I do is more like vagabonding. The differ-ence is subtle, but it's there."

He sneered at me and grasped the gem in his upraised fist. I thought I saw something moving within the gem, like a light darting around inside. If I didn't know any better, I would say the gem was *looking* around the room.

"Go ahead and crack jokes, McCool, but know that I've been planning this day since I first heard you'd moved to the city. The Circle wanted to hunt you down and destroy you as soon as they learned how you murdered your partner. But the old man pulled a few strings and called in a few favors, so the Circle was forced to stand back, and watch.

"But I wasn't about to just sit back and wait for your ríastrad to erupt again—oh no. I've a sworn duty as a

Circle mage to protect the innocent from supernatural dangers of all kinds." He pointed at me with his free hand. "And that means you, McCool, and that damned curse you carry within you. So I waited and planned, and prepared."

I sniffed and stifled a yawn. "Alright, I'll bite—how'd you steal the Tathlum? And furthermore, what's with the gem?"

He chuckled. "My mentor is far more powerful than any Circle mage on the ruling Council, even more powerful than Maeve, I think. Suffice it to say that I had adequate help in getting past her wards and spells."

I nodded. "Fair enough. And the gem?"

He smiled. "You'll see in due time. Any other questions?"

"Are you one of the people behind Ananda Corp and CIRCE?"

He shook his head. "No, that's one of my mentor's projects. It was how we first learned Maeve had been entrusted with the artifact. According to one of the fae we killed, Lugh himself granted it into her possession for safekeeping before the old gods disappeared from the mortal realm."

"Ah, so you were trying to start a war between the Pack and the fae. You failed, you know."

He sneered and curled his lip. "Merely a distraction.

The real plan involved bringing you here, tonight. Everything else was secondary to this moment."

He was completely engrossed in that gem, but I needed to keep him talking while I put the finishing touches on the spell I still had hidden in my hand. So, I kept stroking his ego with questions.

"Why'd you kidnap Sabine? She didn't have anything to do with any of this."

He shrugged. "The time was right. I'd figured out how to crack the Tathlum, and I needed a way to bring you here. Not that you wouldn't have made it here eventually, but—" he gestured around him dramatically, "—timing is everything, you know. And I've been waiting for this moment, for a long, long time."

"Kind of stupid to throw the Dullahan at me then. If it would have killed me, it would have made all this moot."

He cackled and quickly cut his laughter off. "Oh, that wasn't me. Obviously, you're not as well-informed of your enemies as you think."

I nodded to concede the point. He was right, I didn't have a handle on all the players; heck, I didn't even know what the game was, exactly. Still, none of it mattered at the moment, because Sabine and Belladonna were both safe and I was about to get Maeve's rock back so I could get out from under her thumb. Tired of the verbal back and forth, I prepared to release the spell I'd been readying for the last few minutes.

"Well, it's been nice chatting with you, Crowley, and I have to admit that for a sociopath you're actually not a bad guy. But I have homework I've been neglecting and I'd really like to get this over with. So why don't you tell me what that gemstone is?"

He rolled his eyes. "The fae girl was right. You are slow. Let me bring you up to speed, then."

Fae girl?

Crowley clucked his tongue, and the imp carefully folded up his magazine and set it down next to him. He was sitting on the edge of his seat now, grasping the shelf with both hands and looking back and forth between us, like a cat watching a tennis match.

"Oh, this is going to be good," the imp whispered.

"It's time for the big reveal. You ready for this, druid?" He stood up straighter and held the gemstone aloft in his fingers, revealing it to me fully for the first time.

"Behold, the Eye of Balor!"

That's when I knew I was about to get ass-raped with a jackhammer.

FOR THOSE WHO don't know Irish mythology, Balor

was a king among the Fomorians. I might have mentioned that already, but what I didn't mention was that he was also an inspiration for many of the comic book superheroes and villains of our day. See, not only was Balor a giant, massively strong, god-like creature, and likely the monster from whose seed the fachen sprang; he also possessed an insanely destructive magical power that was said to be able to slay entire armies at a glance.

Ever hear the name "Balor of the Evil Eye?" Yeah, well, that's where they got the idea for every superhero power that ever involved shooting anything out of a hero or villain's eyes. According to legend, Balor was the original super-powered badass. With one glance his eyes could burn up forests, melt stone, and catch entire swathes of the countryside on fire. No army was ever said to resist it, and his gaze was powerful enough to slay gods. Nuada, high king of the Tuatha Dé Danann, was killed by Balor's magic laser heat vision. The legends say that Lugh shot out Balor's eye in revenge before beheading him and ending his menace for good.

But now it looked like the legends were a little off. Who knew?

As Crowley held the Eye aloft, I saw that it was an eye. The thing I'd seen moving around inside it was a pupil, a bright orange circle of light surrounded by a glowing red iris. And that thing was looking around the room like the eye of Sauron, presumably searching for targets of opportunity.

Crowley crowed in triumph as he continued his villainous monologue. "You see, Colin, Lugh didn't pierce Balor's eye. He merely knocked him unconscious with his sling. And once he'd beheaded the giant, he plucked that eye out and kept it in reserve as his own personal WMD, just in case another threat ever appeared to match that of the Fomorians. Of course, he created the myth about shooting out Balor's eye to fool those who might want the weapon for themselves."

Crowley polished the gem on his sleeve and admired it. "Personally, I thought hiding it inside the Tathlum was a particularly nice touch."

I smiled. "I appreciate the history lesson—fascinating stuff, really. But I just have one more question for you."

"Sure, whatever. I can wait a few more seconds before I burn you to ash."

Once I had his undivided attention, I plastered the most serious look I could muster across my face and asked: "Tell me, Crowley—can your pussy do the dog?"

"Whah—?" Crowley's brow furrowed as his mind attempted to process the most ridiculous and entertaining question ever asked in the history of punk and rockabilly music. And in that split-second of confusion, I threw the small ball of enchanted ice I'd been hiding with all my might, hoping like hell that the Eye needed a moment or two to rev up before unleashing its power.

Thankfully, my gamble paid off. The ice struck him in his chest and the spell triggered, immediately coating him in a thick covering of hoarfrost and icicles. He instantly froze in place like a statue as I bolted across the circle, pulling a tranquilizer pistol from my coat and firing it at him from a few meters away.

Unfortunately, the imp had flown across the room to protect Crowley as soon as it realized I was attacking its master. Likely being under a geas, it would be bound to defend Crowley with its own life. It hovered in front of Crowley's chest for a moment with the bright-green fletching of the tranquilizer dart quivering in one of its butt cheeks. Then, it fell to the ground with a thud, snoring loudly and drooling with its tongue sticking from its mouth. Apparently, injecting a 20-pound imp with enough M99 to put down a 13,000-pound African bush elephant resulted in near-instantaneous unconsciousness.

To my dismay, that left a temporarily frozen but still very conscious Crowley to deal with, and he did not look happy. Worse yet, the tranq gun held only one dart. As I began backing away, the gemstone in his hand fixed that creepy pupil on me and began to glow.

"Oh, shit!" I yelled, running for the nearest window and hoping I'd land on something soft after falling thirty feet. Anyhow, breaking a leg or two was better than being fried like a bug under a magnifying glass on a sunny day. I was almost to the nearest open window when I felt a tremendous heat on my back. The wards I'd placed on my dad's overcoat flared briefly and shattered under the sheer power of the Eye's magic. Then the concussive force of the Eye's gaze blasted me out the window, straight through the burning ruins of the barn next door.

Fortunately for me, and unfortunately for anything that was stuck inside there with me, my ríastrad had already kicked in before I'd even hit the barn.

AS I FELT the change coming over me, the bottom dropped out of my stomach. Everything was moving in slow motion; I was aware that I was airborne and crashing through the roof and walls of a burning building, but I didn't feel a thing. All I felt was pain—not physical pain, but the emotional kind, and a deep, mind-numbing dread. Every memory of that awful night two years ago came rushing back in a flood, and I relived it all in an instant.

The cave. The dragon. The fight. Jesse's death.

Then the ríastrad took over. Suddenly all that pain and anguish was gone, replaced by an endless rage that rose from a ravenous pool of hate inside me. It had no beginning and no end—it just *was*. I looked at my hands and arms and watched as they began to warp and disfigure. One arm grew hideously larger and more muscular than the other, and yet the smaller arm still bulged with muscles and tendons that strained against my skin until I thought it would burst. My limbs lengthened as they gained girth, and my bones cracked and ground as they shifted and thickened within my body, straining against clothes that stretched and shredded to accommodate my transformation.

My back arched and seized with tremendous pain, and I grew a kyphotic hump in my upper spine that threatened to displace my neck. I felt the bones in my face and skull realign, and groaned as my jaw thickened and lengthened. I raised my hands in front of my face— two monstrous, misshapen things, one a hammer and the other a claw—still with all five fingers and toes, and vaguely human. Thickened, leathery callouses and hard, bony protrusions stuck out of every knuckle.

Finally, I felt the skin all over my body thicken and transform. I grew hair, thick curls of it, from my knuckles, face, chest, and feet. My boots were tattered and hanging from my now massive ankles. I shook them off like a dog shaking its leg after a good long piss, just before I hit the ground. I landed in a corn field like a meteor come to earth and left a deep, dark furrow of freshly turned soil behind me as I slid to a stop some thirty meters beyond where I'd landed.

The rational, human part of me was still inside, but riding along like a passenger. I had no control over my body and no say-so in what would happen next. And that deeper, darker, primal part of me, the one that felt nothing but hate and rage, now sat fully in the driver's seat.

And it wanted *revenge*.

TWENTY-THREE

Journal Entry—9 Months, 25 Days A.J.

After all that trouble we went through to sober him up, it turns out Finn had the alchemical recipe tucked away in one of his grimoires. Wish he would have just told us that in the first place. I can't even stand to look at him, so I'm kind of glad we don't need his help to finish this up. Maureen volunteered to help me prepare the formula, or potion, or whatever you want to call it, and we've been working away in the lab at Finn's warehouse where Jesse and I used to train.

I hadn't been back here since it happened. Cooking and distilling all the various components of an alchemical concoction like this involves a lot of waiting, so I've been roaming around the place remembering old times. There's a layer of dust over everything, but the smell of leather, iron, blood, and sweat stirred up a lot of memo-

ries. *I can still remember the first time she brought me in here; it was right after we defeated the Avartagh. We were just kids then, and it was going to be the adventure of a lifetime.*

If only I'd known then what I know now.

So, tonight's the night—I finally get to see Jesse again. I'll probably be tripping balls when it happens, but still.

I can't wait.

-McC

AUSTIN, Texas—Present Day

I howled Crowley's name into the night, and was answered by a roar that came from my left and behind me, in the direction of the still blazing remains of the barn.

A challenger! My huge, malformed lips parted and my mouth pulled itself into a terrible rictus of a grin. Spittle flew from my lips and my eyes bulged from their sockets. I pivoted toward that sound, screaming obscenities. Something was coming at me, and fast, and the hate inside gleefully welcomed the brawl that was sure to follow.

Thrum... Thrum... THRUM!

Suddenly the fachen collided with me, like a freight train hitting a dump truck. Transformed by the ríastrad I was better than three meters tall, but the fachen was easily half again my height. Yet I was nearly equal its mass because I had four limbs, while it had only one arm and leg attached to its slender half-torso. Still, when the fachen struck, it took me off my feet. I rolled with the force of the collision, coming up in a three-point crouch bellowing my family name as a battle cry.

"MacCumhaill, MacCumhaill, MacCumhaill!" I roared.

Then the beast came at me again, and although I couldn't see it, I could sense it and smell it. It smelled of rotten flesh and death, yet nothing inside me felt the least amount of fear—because pure elemental hate leaves no room for fear. I carried nothing inside but unbridled fury. As I heard the fachen approach again, I focused it all into one mighty punch, digging my toes into the ground for leverage and rotating to drive all my mass behind that great meaty battering ram of a fist.

The timing was perfect. My fist struck the giant and stopped it dead in its tracks, sinking satisfyingly deep into muscle and gristle. As my fist sunk into its torso, I felt something snap with a metallic ping under my knuckles. I assumed it was a charm of some sort, because just then the fachen shimmered into view before me, folded in two over my fist.

Its face had to have been a match for mine in sheer ugliness, because it was twisted and deformed and terrible to behold. It had one eye in the center of its massive forehead, and a shock of thick black feathers on top of its skull in place of hair. I smelled rotting meat as its breath escaped from its mouth, and there were flecks of masticated flesh and clothing stuck between its numerous crooked teeth.

I took in the scene in an instant and continued my assault. But the way I attacked, I wouldn't even call what I was doing "fighting," because that would be too tame a term. As I swung my next blow, words jumbled around inside my head to describe what I intended to do to the fachen:

PulverizeRendTearMaimPummelDismemberMangleMutilateSunderTortureEviscerateDestroyBrutalize... KILL.

And it was all just as natural as breathing to me.

I pivoted ninety degrees and brought that other, claw-like hand down on the side of the fachen's head, ripping skin and tearing its ear clean off its head. I shifted my weight and kicked out with one foot, collapsing the fachen's massive knee and bringing it further down to my level. Then I leapt on top of it and began beating it with both fists in a furious, unrelenting attack.

But the fachen was not going down without a fight. The blood of the Fomorians ran through its veins, and it too was a massive, primal thing made for the same purpose as me: to destroy. As I beat it around the head, neck, and torso, its single arm shifted from one side of its body to the other. In the giant's hand was a flail, so big it looked to have been made from a telephone pole and wrecking ball. It swung the flail at me in a great arc, the spiked ball at the end of the chain colliding with my shoulder and knocking me off its back.

I rolled and came to my feet, facing the monster as it contorted its single arm and leg to get back to its feet.

"Abomination," it rumbled. "Cú Chulainn's curse is fully released upon you, foul man. Your kind were never meant to be."

The fachen spun the flail like a saw blade as it spoke, so fast it became a blur. "You'll meet your end this night by my hand, as so many men have in years gone by, and the resting gods will thank me from their slumber for ridding the world of your blasphemous presence."

The creature's words registered, but I cared little for their meaning. I popped my shoulder back into socket and growled my reply.

"Less talk, more pain, Fomorian."

Heedless of the spinning metal ball at the end of that chain, I flung myself at the beast. I collided with it before it could attack and drove it through the smoldering remains of the barn. We continued out the other side and crashed into the silo, denting it severely. The structure tottered precariously a few seconds before tipping completely. It landed in an adjacent field amidst a chorus of screeching metal and shattered glass and wood.

We staggered apart for a moment, recovering to circle each other in the gravel drive before clashing and trading blows once, twice, and a third time, with me getting the worst of those exchanges. Finally, due to our difference in height, I was forced to change tactics and grapple with it—an awkward proposition against a giant half-again my size with just one arm and one leg.

I dodged a blow from the flail and climbed up on the creature's back, wrapping my legs around its torso and holding on with one arm while beating it senseless. It staggered and fell into a decrepit tractor near the burning barn, with the force of our combined mass bending the tractor's frame around us. I continued pummeling the beast with my fists until it shifted its arm to its upper back, swinging the flail overhead and smashing it into my skull. I staggered as it struck me over and over again, driving me to my knees.

Shrugging the broken remains of the tractor off, it towered over me as I attempted to get back to my feet. The fachen spat blood, then bent that single mighty leg and leapt straight up, ten feet or more in the air, intending to smash me underfoot. I rolled from underneath, stumbling to a nearby fence where I snatched two posts from the ground with their concrete footings still intact.

Now I'd have some fun.

The fachen leapt at me with a speed that belied its size, swinging the flail at my body. I blocked the flail with one fence post, and it shattered with the impact. At the same time, I swung the other at the creature's upper arm. The arm snapped with a loud crack, bending at an unnatural angle to hang uselessly at the giant's side. It cried out in agony.

"Balor should have given his children two arms and legs," I growled as I struck it in the face with the fence-post. Without the use of its single arm it was helpless to defend itself, and realized it had been defeated. No longer interested in battle, the fachen fled with its broken arm flopping behind it.

"Come back here!" I roared. "I'm not finished with you yet!" I threw the fencepost at it and missed, then looked about the area for something else to use as a projectile weapon. Near the wrecked tractor was a large metal grader blade, a tractor attachment used for leveling soil and gravel. I snagged it with both hands and pivoted like a decathlete throwing the discus, getting up to speed before letting it fly. The metal blade spun through the air like a Frisbee in a flat, straight trajectory that caught the fachen at the waist in mid-leap, severing it in two.

I walked over to the creature, picking up the discarded fencepost on the way. Its pelvis and leg bled and twitched in the dirt just a few yards from the torso and head. It struggled for breath as I approached, wheezing and shuddering as its entrails spilled out on the ground.

The fachen's eye fixed on me as I lumbered up to it, and it cursed me with its final agonized breath. "May your ríastrad consume you, Irishman, and every person you hold dear."

"Too late for that, peg-leg," I growled. "It already has." I raised the fence post like a mace overhead, smashing it down on the giant's skull over and over again, until the ground was stained red and nothing but pulp remained.

When the bloody task was done, my thoughts cleared and I recalled there was another, more dangerous enemy present. A black rage welled up from within me as my eyes searched the night for the wizard.

"You're next, Crowley!" I roared. "You hear me? You're next!"

I DIDN'T HAVE to search long to find the wizard; he found me first. He stumbled from the wreckage of the silo, and as soon as I spotted him he released the full fury of the Eye on me. The blast hit me squarely in the chest, burning what remained of my clothes from my torso and searing me with its heat. I flew back several feet, rolled head over heels, and came up to one knee.

Crowley stalked toward me, only staggering slightly as he walked me down. He raised the Eye and struck again, but this time I held both hands up to shield my face and body, roaring in agony as the pain from the blast heated my hands. Thankfully, it appeared that each blast was limited in duration, so they only lasted a few seconds at a time. I somehow withstood that blast, but the heat and the force of it laid me flat. I groaned in pain and anger and came up on my elbows, panting with the exertion.

The wizard stopped several feet from me, wisely out of range of a kick or a wild swing. He was covered in sheetrock dust and blood, and his clothes were as tattered and torn as mine. His eyes looked wild, and shadows whipped around him as he prepared to loose his magic along with that of Balor's Eye.

"Finally, McCool, the world will be free from your curse." He raised the stone for what I knew would be the final blow. I was no longer able to protect myself; my chest was a smoking, charred wreck, and my hands were blackened and twisted from defending his most recent attack.

I stared into the Eye, meeting its gaze with my own for the first time. As it glowed hotter and hotter, I prepared for my own end. I felt no remorse in my transformed state, only hate, and inside I vowed that I would take revenge from the grave if necessary. An empty oath, because I knew that ghosts had little power to affect the physical realm.

But the part of me that was human—the thinking, rational part of me—that part sighed in relief. Soon, it would be over, and I'd be able to rejoin Jesse in the next life. I lifted my head and looked up at the wizard.

"Do it. *Do it*, coward!"

Then a voice rumbled all around us.

NO.

It took us both a moment to realize that the voice came from the stone. It flew out of Crowley's grasp and floated in the air between us.

FOR MILLENNIA I HAVE WAITED TO HAVE MY REVENGE ON LUGH AND HIS KIND. HIS MAGIC HELD MY WILL AT BAY. NOW I AM RELEASED, AND THIS ONE'S DESIRES DO NOT SUIT MY OWN.

Crowley reached out for the Eye to grab it, and it flared brilliantly with heat and light. He snatched his hand back with a cry, and tucked it blistered and burned against his chest.

The wizard screamed with impotent fury at the Eye.

"But I released you! I did it, and no one else. It was my plan. Mine. How dare you defy my will?"

I AM NOT A GOD. BUT I ONCE CHAN-

NELED A GOD'S POWER. WHO ARE YOU TO DEFY MY WILL, HUMAN?

The Eye flared again and blasted Crowley's form, but this time he was ready for it. Shadow magic wrapped around him as he cringed away, absorbing some of the blast and cushioning his fall as the power of the Eye flung him meters away into a pile of gravel and dirt. He landed in a twisted and unconscious heap, a partially charred rag doll missing half the skin on his face.

The Eye swiveled back to me. The rational part of me reflected upon how much I hated sentient magical objects. But the living hate within took great pleasure at seeing Crowley brought low. A laugh rumbled from my misshapen lips.

YOU REVEL IN PAIN AND DESTRUCTION. I WISH TO DESTROY THE LAST REMNANT OF THE TUATHA DÉ DANANN. WHAT BETTER CREATURE TO WIELD ME?

At that, the Eye floated toward me, rapidly increasing in speed until it struck me in the forehead. I felt a searing, unbearable pain, like a red hot poker was being forced through my skull. Then, I lapsed into unconsciousness.

TWENTY-FOUR

JournalEntry—9 Months, 27 Days A.J.

Well, it looks like Jesse is going to stick around for a while. I'll write more about it later, after I've had a chance to process what went down last night.

-McC

AUSTIN, Texas—Present Day

I awoke just as the first tendrils of light were peeking out over the fields of corn nearby, and sat up to take stock in my situation. I was nearly naked, and only a few tattered shreds remained of the pants I was wearing the night previous. My hands were swollen, red, and tender, but thankfully not the blackened and charred slabs of meat they'd been a few hours before. All the hair had been singed off my chest, but other than a circular red mark that resembled a bad sunburn, I was fine.

The barn was nothing but ash, and the silo was lying on its side halfway across a cornfield, with one side smashed in to bear evidence of the fight I'd had with the fachen earlier. The fachen's corpse was gone, as was Crowley, and despite searching the property I found neither hide nor hair of him or his imp. However, my search did turn up my Craneskin Bag, and although the shoulder strap was torn, it was otherwise undamaged. After rummaging around inside for a spare set of clothes and some Chuck Taylors, I tied a knot in the strap and slung it over my shoulder.

By the time I got dressed, Belladonna was running toward me from the direction of the front gate, along with a squad of Circle hunters and wizards. Bells ran up to me and looked me over, checking me for wounds or other signs of injury. After a brief head to toe assessment, she sighed in relief and stepped back, just as her back up approached with a tall gray-haired man in the lead. He was dressed in urban digicam fatigues, and looked a bit like Sam Elliott did in that *Hulk* movie, the crappy one with Eric Bana.

"You must be McCool. I'm Field Commander Gunnarson, obviously of the Cold Iron Circle. Where in the hell is my rogue wizard, McCool? And what in the name of Freya's gilded tits happened here?" Huh, he kind of talked like Elliott, too.

I glanced over his shoulder at Belladonna, who was now standing at parade rest just behind him and to his left. She shook her head ever so slightly, warning me not to say anything about what had happened.

"I really don't know, sir. He was trying to complete some ritual and I attempted to stop him. The last thing I remember was being flung from the window of that silo over there." I pointed at the wreckage and tried to look shell-shocked, which was pretty easy to do at the moment.

The Circle commander tongued his cheek. "Uh-huh. And you expect me to believe that you survived an attack from a wizard in possession of an ancient magical artifact, as well as that wizard's hired Fomorian giant— all without going to the dark side again? Just what kind of stupid do you think I am, son?"

"The Cold Iron Circle kind, sir?"

That didn't go over well. A vein started to throb in the middle of Gunnarson's forehead, and his lip curled up at the corner of his mouth. One of his eyebrows started twitching, and I knew I'd struck nerve. He got up in my face and started yelling, spitting flecks of chewing tobacco spit in my face as he spoke.

"Oh, you want to play games with me, druid? Let me

tell you, son, I got more games than Milton-fucking-Bradley and more time to play them than Father-fucking-Time! Now, you will tell me exactly what happened here, or I will personally ream your ass so hard and long, you'll think you got raped by a gods-damned jotunn!"

Belladonna chose that moment to try to take some of the heat—bad move on her part. Not that I didn't appreciate it.

"Um, sir, I believe I can explain—"

Gunnarson turned his steely gaze on her and spoke in a deep, calm voice. "Becerra, as usual your verbal interjections are just like cancer. Slow, sure, and completely fucking unwanted. If I want your opinion, I will tell you what it is. Is that understood?"

Her face turned beet red, and she nodded. "Completely, sir."

That really ticked me off. He could dress me down all he wanted, but there was no way I was letting him talk that way to my friend.

"You know what, Field Commander Gunnarson? You're an asshole. Now let's get one thing clear. I don't work for the Circle, and I don't answer to the Circle. If you think I've done something wrong, then you're going to have to apprehend me—good luck with that.

"But even then, if you somehow manage to take me in without triggering one of my 'episodes,'" I made quotes in the air with my fingers as I said it, "then you're going to have to answer to Luther, and I don't think you're prepared to kick that particular hornet's nest."

Gunnarson's fists clenched and his eyes tightened. He gestured to the squad of a half-dozen wizards and hunters who'd accompanied him onto the property. "Restrain this man," he stated coldly.

Just then, a sleek black limousine rolled up the gravel drive and came along beside us. The Circle hunters and wizards paused, checking to see who it might be and whether or not they would be a threat. As the car pulled to a stop, the rear window rolled down, and Maeve's voice echoed from the back of the car.

"Commander, a word." He scowled and walked over to the car's window. There was a brief, hushed conversation between them, then the window rolled back up and the car pulled away. The commander watched it drive off into the distance, and when he turned around his face was etched with frustration.

"Strike team, belay that order. McCool, you're free to go." He spared me one final glance, then he strode off in a huff, screaming orders and obscenities at his team and sending them to and fro to secure the scene. Belladonna gave me a look of regret, then followed close on his heels.

I looked around once and decided I'd had enough of

these Cold Iron Circle clowns for one day. Pointedly ignoring the Circle hunters and wizards, I shuffled down the gravel drive to retrieve Sal's car, whistling The Cramps' *Goo Goo Muck* the whole way.

I KNEW I couldn't put off my meeting with Maeve forever, but decided that it was no good to try explaining what had happened on just a few hours of sleep. So, after heading back to the junkyard and sleeping till noon, I got up, dressed, and headed for her house.

When I arrived, there was a ruby red Porsche Panamera parked in the driveway. The license plates read "FAEDIVA"—I could only assume it belonged to Siobhán. For one, Maeve never drove anywhere, and second she'd never be so droll as to have customized license plates. If I'd only noticed the plates back at CIRCE, it would have saved me a hell of a lot of trouble. *Hmpf.*

As I headed up the front walk, of course the troll was nowhere to be seen. In its place were two gargoyles, perched atop a pair of pillars that framed the entrance to a stone terrace that hadn't been there on my last visit. The stonework didn't look new at all, but instead had a convincingly weathered appearance. If I didn't know any better, I would have thought it had been there for decades. The gargoyles, true to form, remained completely still, but their stone eyes followed me all the way to the entrance.

When I rang the doorbell, it was answered by none other than Siobhán. She was dressed more elegantly this time, in a long, front slit skirt that hugged her figure from hips to ankles, and a clingy, open-backed top that revealed more skin than it covered. She opened the door and stretched one arm lazily up the doorframe, resting her cheek against her shoulder and gazing at me with heavy-lidded eyes.

"Colin, what a pleasant surprise—Maeve will be so pleased. Do come in." She turned and sashayed into the house, bearing a tight-lipped smile like the cat who ate the bird and got away with it.

I cleared my throat. "I ran into a friend of yours last night."

She looked over her shoulder. "Really? And who might that be? I wouldn't think we'd move in the same circles."

I tilted my head. "Meh, I'm full of surprises. It was your buddy, Crowley—he said to say hi if I saw you."

She sniffed and turned away. "Can't say the name rings a bell."

"C'mon, Siobhán," I countered. "I know you're involved. I saw your car pulling out of CIRCE the other day, and I saw you speeding off from the junkyard the night of the attack."

She barely raised an eyebrow, as if she couldn't be bothered to exert herself. "Now, Colin, Maeve is far too invested in you at the moment for me to go against her wishes and send that dreary old harbinger after you. And as far as this 'Circe' person you speak of, I have no idea who you're talking about."

I smiled, but my eyes were cold as ice.

"I didn't say anything about what attacked us, Siobhán—to *anyone*." Her brow furrowed ever so slightly. *Game point, bitch.* But despite the fact that she'd been caught, she gave not the slightest indication she was vexed by my accusations.

"Perhaps I assumed, then. Come along." She turned on heel and strutted off, adopting a swaybacked gait that almost made it worth it to be in her presence. Almost.

I snickered and followed her through a few more rooms into a study, where Maeve was sitting in front of a very old, very expensive antique desk. She was wearing a pair of reading glasses that I doubted she needed, and was studying a large, ancient tome. When I tried to decipher the writing on the page she was reading, the letters squiggled and blurred and simply made my head hurt. We waited for her to finish whatever she'd been looking at, and she closed the book. My headache immediately receded.

"Thank you for escorting our guest to me, Siobhán. You may be excused."

Siobhán curtsied slightly before leaving the room. She didn't even spare me a parting glance. *Huh, must be losing my touch.* I waited until she was out of hearing range.

"Siobhán was involved, somehow. I can't prove it, but I'm certain of it."

Maeve nodded as she turned to face me. "I already knew as much." She gestured to an easy chair nearby. "Have a seat, Colin."

I sat as she swiveled her work chair to face me, steepling her fingers and gazing at me long enough to make me nervous. Finally, she spoke.

"It seems we have a problem, Colin. You've recovered the stone, correct?"

I tilted my head and squinted. "Eh, what was left of it, anyway."

"And yet, you are unable to return it to me. Is that also correct?"

I shook my head. "No, not at the moment, I'm afraid."

She studied me again over her fingers, and then spread her hands and laid them on her thighs, leaning forward and smiling slightly as she did so.

"Well, I can't say that I'm not disappointed, but I knew that this might happen. However, the fact remains that you failed to come through on your end of our bargain."

I did a double-take. "Wait a minute—you *knew* that the Eye might decide to embed itself in my head?"

Her mouth turned up slightly, and her eyes crinkled around the edges. "I knew it was a possibility, and I considered it to be a calculated risk. But, no harm done, and you don't seem any worse for the wear."

"Maeve, I have a sentient magical artifact residing inside my head—that's hardly something I care to classify as 'no harm done.' What if this thing decides to go off and level a city block?"

She shrugged. "Doubtful. It didn't exactly choose *you* as its bearer, did it? No, it chose that other you, the one it found to be most suited to its purposes. So, unless you decide to let that side of you out, you have nothing to worry about."

I gripped the edges of the easy chair in an effort to keep from raising my voice to the Queen of the Austin Fae. "With all due respect, I fail to see how this is a worry-free situation."

She clucked like a mother comforting her son after a scraped knee. "Now, now, these things happen. We'll just have to keep an eye on it until it shows up again, and then I'll figure out a way to get the Eye back, and safely in my hands.

"But until that time, I'll consider you to have an

unfulfilled debt. And, should I require your services, I'll expect you to continue to perform certain duties for me, until such time as I retrieve my property and release you from my service."

I sighed softly. "Somehow, I feel like this may have been your plan all along."

"Nonsense. No one could have foretold that this would happen. My own seers thought it a mere 2.69 percent possibility that the Eye would choose to bond with your other self. Those are hardly odds that I would stake all our futures upon."

I cocked my head and narrowed my gaze. "What do you mean, 'all our futures'?"

She tittered and covered her mouth with one hand, back once more to playing the charming hostess. "Oh, now, don't worry that handsome little head of yours over things that are above your pay grade."

She turned back to her desk and laid a hand on the book. "Now, I have things to which I must attend. If I have need of you, I'll send word. Siobhán will show you out."

And with that, I was dismissed.

BELLS ENDED up in deep shit with her higher ups in the Cold Iron Circle. Those pricks worked her day and night, sending her on shitty-ass details like chasing down a semi-sentient sewer slime that had been eating cats and dogs near the Drag. It was too small to be of any threat to humans, but they'd had her stalking the public drainage tunnels every night since the fight at Crowley's farm. So, I hadn't seen much of her since then.

Crowley fell off the face of the earth. Belladonna said they hadn't found a single trace of him anywhere on the property, except for some blood on a mound of dirt and gravel that matched his DNA and magical signature. Rumor had it there was evidence of a spatial disturbance nearby, which might have indicated that he or someone else had opened a portal out of there that night. If so, apparently they took the fachen's corpse with them. It was all very, very suspicious, and it smacked of there being serious players involved. Maybe Crowley hadn't been blowing smoke about his mentor being a super-badass wizard... but who knew? I was just glad the prick was out of my hair.

Hemi ended up with a concussion, but otherwise he was fine. Turns out his people had some serious battle juju, and because of all that skin art he was hella hard to kill. I felt like I owed him, though, for sticking his neck out for me like that. So, I agreed to treat him to some brews and barbecue and help him hunt down some body parts for his new ride. He was stoked about it, which was alright by me. Hemi was a good person, and I sure didn't mind having a six-foot-five-inch Maori warrior watching my back.

Samson was happy that I'd stopped Crowley before he killed any more of the Pack—or, for that matter, any more fae. He said Crowley had probably used his magic to briefly paralyze them while the Dullahan did the dirty work. It sounded like a horrible way to die to me. Samson agreed. Unfortunately, they never recovered the heads. They moved the bodies to an underground vault until such time as the Pack could give them a proper burial. The official story was that the 'thropes who died were on loan to another Pack.

Finn stayed true to his word, and had been clean since the night we fought the Dullahan in the junkyard. I had a chat with the red caps when I returned Sal's car, and we came to an understanding that included them supplying Finn with Suboxone until he was completely off the junk. I also got him hooked up with a drug addiction counselor through Dr. Larsen's office. He wasn't quite as obnoxious as he had been, but still wasn't the same old pipe-smoking college professor I remembered from my youth. Maureen said it was common for mortals who lived an excessively long time to go through personality changes every several decades. She claimed it was the only way a mortal mind could deal with immortality.

And Sabine? She was a glaistig with multiple neuroses, so it was hard to say with her. That being said, she seemed to have come through her experience relatively unscathed. However, I noticed that she'd been turning up the juice on her glamour and see-me-not spell, which really bummed me out considering all the progress she'd made.

Currently, she and I were sitting in Luther's place enjoying a cup of coffee and playing checkers like a couple of old people. She was kicking my ass, and had crowned three of her black pieces to just one of my red, and had a stack of red checkers on her side of the board. I was basically just stalling to delay the inevitable at this point.

She waggled her eyebrows at me. "So, are you ready to admit defeat?"

"Alright, you win." I cleared the board and began setting up my pieces again. I got a few weird looks from the other patrons, so I pointed to my earpiece.

"I'm playing with my friend in virtual reality." That got me off the hook and everyone went back to what they were doing. Never mind that I wasn't even wearing VR glasses. People always believed what they wanted to believe.

"So, what do you think Maeve has in store for you?" she asked as she neatly centered each of her pieces on a square.

"I'm not sure, but I have a feeling there's a much bigger game at play, and I'm just being used as a pawn." I picked up a red game piece and flipped it back and forth between my fingers.

"One thing's for sure, though: Maeve and Finn have both hinted that something really bad is on the horizon. That means we need to be ready for it when it comes."

I thought back to what Samson had said about helping me learn to control the ríastrad, and what that might mean. Right now I couldn't even think about losing control, for fear that I might hurt Sabine, or Belladonna, or who knew who else. I sure couldn't go through life wondering if I was going to lose it and kill one of my friends, and it certainly didn't look like I was going to be rid of this curse any time in the near future. Which meant I'd need to go see Samson to discuss his offer—very, very soon.

I flicked the game piece up in the air, and watched as it landed perfectly on top of one of Sabine's black pieces with a satisfying click. *Two opposites, perfectly matched.* I wondered whether that could be a metaphor for my split personality, or for where things might be headed on the relationship front. Who knew? Honestly, the way things had turned out I felt a small bit of hope for the first time since Jesse died. Anything was possible.

I felt the tiniest breeze on my neck and shivered slightly. I looked around to see if someone was standing behind me, or if there was a door or window open, but the room was buttoned up tight and no one was there but us.

Sabine looked up from the board and stared at me quizzically. "Everything okay, Colin?"

I nodded. "Everything's fine, Sabine. Game on."

EPILOGUE

EPILOGUE

The McCool Home—In the Space Between This World and the Next, 9 Months, 26 Days A.J.

"Hey there, slugger."

I opened my eyes, and I was still in my old room in Mom's basement, but somehow I *wasn't* there. Everything was the same, but ethereal and semi-solid looking.

And Jesse was standing there in front of me.

"It's you, isn't it? It's really you?"

She nodded. "It's me, one hundred percent. I've been here since the fight with the Caoránach."

I began crying, although I wasn't sure how that worked here. The last thing I remembered was drinking Finn's magical mystery potion and lying down in bed. I started blubbering like a fool.

"I'm sorry, Jesse—I'm so, so sorry." Then she was there, holding me in her arms.

"Shhh, it's alright. I've heard your apologies a thousand times already, and I forgave you the moment it happened. When I saw the transformation come over you, I figured it was the Caoránach's magic, and I knew it wasn't your fault."

"It was Fúamnach. She sent a messenger to your funeral to gloat."

Jesse nodded. "We don't have much time. We can spend it rehashing the past, or we can have one last perfect night together. Which do you prefer?"

"I just want to stay here with you, forever and ever."

Her eyes softened and she touched my cheek. "You can't, Colin. Your time's not done yet. In fact, *our* time isn't done yet, either. We were supposed to do something important together, something pivotal. But when Fúamnach's curse happened, it threw everything out of whack. That's why I'm still here."

"But what could we possibly have to do that's so important? I've tried to end my life a dozen times so I could be with you, and there's no escape for me. Now you're stuck in between worlds because we have some cosmic duty? That's bullshit, Jesse. No one should have to suffer this much."

"It is what it is, slugger. We didn't have to volunteer to fight the forces of evil. That was our choice. If we hadn't accepted that mantle, someone else would have taken our places. But we did, and what's done is done. Now, we can only deal with the consequences."

I was torn, because a part of me wanted to rail against fate and another just wanted to cherish what little time I had to be with her. "It's not fair."

"Of course it's not, silly. That's life. Just know that I'm not going anywhere, and I'll be there when the time comes for us to do what we need to do."

"Like a guardian angel?"

"Just like that."

I nodded. "Okay. But you have to stop trying to communicate with me. Otherwise you'll fade away into nothing, and then we'll never be together."

She laughed, and it sounded like wind chimes at night. "I know the rules, silly. They told me before I came back. It'll be okay."

"Alright, I can accept that." I looked around the room and back at her. "What now?"

She grinned a crooked little grin that said she was up to no good. "Now, we spend what little time we have making up for all the time we've been apart."

I took her in my arms, and it was just like the first time, all over again.

— — —

This concludes the first volume in the Junkyard Druid series... click here to get the second Colin McCool book,

Graveyard Druid! And there's more Colin waiting for you at my website! Go to MDMassey.com now to download your FREE novel, *Druid Blood: A Junkyard Druid Prequel*. When you do, you'll be subscribed to my newsletter, *and* you'll be the first to find out when the next Colin McCool novel hits bookstore shelves.

BOOK EXCERPT: GRAVEYARD DRUID

Want to know what happens next in the Colin McCool saga? Here's a preview from the next Junkyard Druid novel... Graveyard Druid!

Chapter One

So here I was, stripped down to my skivvies and standing in a makeshift fighting ring in Rendon Park, ready to go mano a mano with a troll. And just how had I ended up here?

A few days ago, I'd gotten a call from Siobhan, granddaughter of the local fae queen Maeve many generations removed. Maeve had recently connived a way to get me under her thumb. She'd cornered the market on my mom's art pieces, threatening to ruin her career by flooding the market and devaluing her work.

That was, if I didn't agree to become her errand boy and enforcer. Why she didn't get one of her fae hunters to do this work was beyond me; I supposed it had something to do with the fact that I was druid-trained, and sort of a neutral figure in the supernatural world.

Plus, you could bet that Maeve had plans and machinations spanning the course of centuries; she was fae, after all. I had a sneaking suspicion that somehow I was a key figure in those plans, at least for the foreseeable future. Her favorite chess piece. Lucky me.

After enjoying a few blessed weeks of relative peace and quiet, Siobhan had called me out of the blue, saying that Maeve had a job for me. I'd had plenty of time to recover after the huge battle I'd won against Crowley, a rogue Circle wizard who'd decided it was his mission in life to put me six feet under.

I couldn't have cared less about Crowley; I'd only been there to retrieve Maeve's magic whatzit, which turned out to be Balor's Eye. Yes, *the* Balor's eye, an artifact powerful enough to vaporize entire armies at a glance. Crowley had stolen it from Maeve in an effort to put me down once and for all. During the battle I'd killed his hired help, a mean-ass giant known as a fachen, and the Eye had put a hurt on Crowley. I won, they lost, and I ended up with a sentient magical gemstone embedded inside my skull. Temporally displaced, of course, which was the best thing I could say about the entire situation.

As it turned out, I'd also killed the son of a troll clan chief while making my way to kicking Crowley's ass. Okay, so I hadn't kicked his ass, the Eye had—but let's not get technical here. Anyway, the troll I'd killed belonged to a tribe that had served Maeve for centuries, and he'd betrayed her by turning coat for Crowley. Now, the trolls were looking to save face, or regain their honor —or whatever trolls did to make amends when they screwed up.

Apparently, that involved bare-knuckle brawling in your skivvies. Thus, my current situation. I stood in an earthen circle, roughly ten meters wide. Stones marked out the makeshift ring, spaced about a foot apart, all the way around. The dirt beneath my bare feet was hard and dry, and I fully expected to get a nasty road rash and dust in every crack and crevice before this thing was done.

Their chief, who I'd taken to calling Ookla since I couldn't pronounce his full name, patted me down to make sure I didn't have a longsword hidden in my Calvin Kleins. As he searched me I reflected on my life choices, recalling that just a few weeks ago I'd been in similar situation, but facing a werewolf. One could easily challenge my sanity and intelligence at the moment, but at least after I was dead, no one would ever be able to say I'd backed down from a fight.

It's the little things that make life worth living.

"Okay, you know the rules. Two enter, one gets schooled. Trolls get honor either way, you get killed still happy day. Okay?"

The chief's lumpy mug curled into a grin that might have been friendly, but instead came across as creepy and evil. Still, I was kind of getting to like the guy. He was in a tough spot, because his kid had screwed up royally by betraying Maeve. He was honor-bound to seek retribution for his son's death, and also to restore goodwill with the kid's former employer. It didn't seem like any of the Toothshank clan held it against me that I'd killed the kid—to the trolls, that was just the cost of crossing their employer. Their real concern was restoring their honor and reputation.

And, for some strange reason, that meant they had to prove their clan's strength by fighting Maeve's representative. Namely, me. Siobhan had conveniently forgotten to tell me all this before she'd sent me to smooth things over. One of these days, I'd put her in her place, hopefully by proving to Maeve that her great-granddaughter was plotting against her.

At present, though, I had more pressing matters. I rolled my shoulders out and nodded. "Let's get this over with, Ookla."

He smiled that creepy smile of his again, then chopped the air with his hand and shouted something in trollish that I assumed meant, "Let the kumite begin!"

I LOOKED across the ring as the chief stepped out of the way. My opponent was closing in fast; trolls were deceptively quick for all their height and mass. Lean and lanky, his body was covered in long, ropy muscles under gray-green skin mottled with warts, moles, and what could only be described as tumors. But the worst thing about trolls was their smell.

The run-in I'd had with the chief's son and his buddy had been no picnic, mainly because Crowley hadn't used any magic to cover up their odor. And troll odor was bad—I mean, just awful. It smelled like necrotic flesh, feces, and foot stank, and had the same effects on the respiratory system and mucous membranes as military-grade tear gas. When Belladonna and I had jumped them, we'd nearly been incapacitated by their funk. My friend Sabine, who we were there to rescue, had been knocked unconscious by the stench. It was that bad. And I was going to have to get up close and personal with this thing.

To their credit, the trolls understood what a powerful weapon their reek was. The chief had taken countermeasures to make sure the fight was fair. The clan's witch doctor had cast a spell on me to protect me from the odor, saying it was "good juju, no boohoo you." Obviously, that cat knew his stuff, because I couldn't smell a damned thing, and I mean nothing. Besides that, my sinuses were more clear than they'd been in weeks, and with all the pollen we had to deal with year-round in Austin, that was saying something.

But still, I was going to need a magical tomato juice bath after this match. And, I'd probably have to burn anything that came into contact with the troll's skin. Meaning, my underwear were going to be buried at sea while I bathed in the river after the match.

That is, if I survived. My opponent looked like he meant business. He came forward in a low stance, similar to some Southern kung-fu and karate styles I'd seen. He had one hand in a high guard by his head, the other low and bent across his waist. His lead hand was in a fist; the other was open, fingers extended into a spear. That likely meant the lead hand was his shield, and the rear hand was his intended weapon. Good to know.

He kept inching in, closer and closer. I assumed that meant he was trying to get in range to throw that spear-hand at my eyes or solar plexus. Instead of staying in place, I danced around him like Bruce Lee—and I mean literally like Bruce Lee, cat cries and all. All that show-boating wasn't worth a lick for fighting, but I figured it might confuse him and cause him to make a mistake. We moved around for a minute or so like that, me dancing and making "waa-taah!" sounds as he kept edging in.

Finally, I got bored and decided to draw him out. I did a pendulum step in, rapidly replacing my front foot with my back, and snapped a roundhouse kick at his lead knee. Surprisingly, my kick connected, but it felt like kicking a steel pole wrapped in foam rubber. My instep bounced off his leg after the initial jolting impact. Before I could dance back out of the way, his spearhand darted at my face. I slipped and parried, and his fingertips creased the side of my forehead. I felt a trickle of blood run down my cheek as I moved back, out of range.

The trolls around the ring cheered.

My foot throbbed from the impact I'd made with the troll's knee. That was the thing with trolls; they were tough. Skin like leather, flesh like rubber, and bones like steel. And, they healed fast. To kill one, you basically had to behead it and then incinerate it. I had no weapons at the moment, nor was I allowed to use magic, otherwise this joker's head would have already been flying and frying. I'd just have to improvise.

I danced around a few more seconds, feigning an injury in my foot. It hurt, sure, but it was still functional. Even so, the pain made it easy to put on a good show. As I did, I allowed myself to drift just a little too close to the troll. As expected, he used that opportunity to attack again, spearing his fingers at my eyes.

As soon as he moved, I shifted my stance to face him and lowered my weight, ducking under his attack. In the same motion, I dove forward into a tackle, driving my shoulder into the troll's stomach while grabbing his legs and pulling them in close. After that, it was just a matter of leverage and forward momentum. I had the troll pinned on his back in a flash, sitting on his chest with a knee on either side of his body.

A collective gasp came from the crowd of trolls around the ring, and they began to chatter excitedly amongst themselves. The noise barely registered, though; I was busy putting a beatdown on the troll, with open-handed strikes that landed all around his face and neck. My gamble had paid off. This troll didn't know shit about grappling, and it was obvious he wasn't a fan of the UFC, either. He tried to push me off as he took the first dozen blows or so, but he might as well have been trying to move the Rock of Gibraltar. I could have used the opportunity to slap on an armbar, but the troll would just pop his elbow straight again and heal within seconds.

No, I needed something that would take him out completely. I kept striking him, waiting for him to cover his head with both arms. I continued to hammer him, aiming blows at wherever I saw an opening. A few seconds later he did exactly what I expected, rolling and covering the back of his head with his hands, guarding the sides of his head with his folded arms.

Now I had him.

I wrapped my legs around his body and hooked my heels in his groin, both for better purchase and to kick him in the balls as a distraction. I pummeled him mercilessly from his back until he gave me an opening, then quickly snaked my hand and arm under his chin and back around the other side of his head. I grabbed my biceps on my other arm and secured the rear naked choke, what the Brazilians call "the lion killer." And I squeezed, counting to twenty slowly in my head.

At the end of my count, he was out like a light. Instead of killing him, I rolled him onto his back, picking up his arm and letting it flop to the ground to show the crowd I'd dispatched their champion. I placed a foot on his chest and raised my arms in the air for good measure.

The crowd and chieftain went silent, all of them staring at me with what looked like anger and disbelief. I was getting nervous. In seconds, the troll I'd fought would come around, and then I'd probably have to fight him again. I was exhausted after the match, and didn't know if I had the juice to take him out a second time.

The chieftain shouted something in trollish, and the crowd erupted in cheers. They rushed the ring, vaulting me up on their shoulders and carrying me around the circle, chanting trollish rhymes and making one hell of a ruckus. I worried that we might draw a crowd. We were all glamoured, but the noise they made had me nervous just the same.

In the confusion, I managed to catch a glimpse of my opponent. He had sat up, attended to by the witch doctor. They exchanged a few words, but I couldn't hear what they said. He finally nodded, locking eyes with me, mouth set in a grim expression. After a brief, uncomfortable moment, he cracked a grin and placed a closed fist over his chest in what I assumed was acquiescence of his defeat. Then he stood and pushed through the crowd, joining the fray by hoisting me up on his shoulders.

I was really going to have to burn my undies after this.

Want more?
Get Graveyard Druid at Amazon.com now!

ABOUT THE AUTHOR

I write dark fantasy, paranormal suspense, and urban fantasy novels.

My first series, THEM, is a jaunt through a post-apocalyptic central Texas where the dead walk, and vampires, werewolves and other unsavory creatures roam the night. It has elements of the zompoc genre, dark fantasy, and military survival fiction.

On the other hand, my Colin McCool series falls squarely between urban fantasy and paranormal suspense. Colin's world is full of magic, mystery, and folklore come to life.

I currently live in the Hill Country near Austin, Texas, which is where much of my fiction is set. Most days you can find me in a local coffee shop or in my office working on my next book, or in my garage pummeling inanimate objects. If you'd like to find out more about my work and get a FREE ebook, visit my website at MDMassey.com.

 facebook.com/mdmasseyauthor

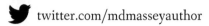 twitter.com/mdmasseyauthor

instagram.com/authormdmassey

Made in the USA
Las Vegas, NV
24 September 2022